Island Of Regrets

By Lee Thompson

Copyright 2013 Lee Thompson
All Rights Reserved
ISBN 1484861159
ISBN-13 978-1484861158

This book is a work of fiction. The characters, incidents, and dialogue are drawn from the author's imagination and are not to be construed as real. Any resemblance to actual events or persons, living or dead, is entirely coincidental.

All rights reserved. No part of this book may be used or reproduced in any manner whatsoever without written permission from the author/publisher, except in the case of brief quotations embodied in critical articles and reviews.

Dedicated to my wife Teri for putting up with me through the writing of this story. She knows too well that it took several months, and she made sure the house stayed in shape the entire time.

Acknowledgements

Thank you Teri for the support, the encouragement, and for putting up with me not being available for hours at a time.

Thank you Teri and Ruthane, without your editing help, the story would still be a mess.

Thank you Nicola Trwst and Kristine Cayne, without your help, this story would not contain any French.

Thank you to my friends and family who gave me the encouragement and support to finish.

> Dear, it took so long just to feel alright
> Remember how to put back the light in my eyes
> I wish I had missed the first time that we kissed
> Cause you broke all your promises
> - Jar Of Hearts by Christina Perry

Michelle woke to the sound of ocean surf. A gentle breeze caressed her short hair. Sunlight filtering through vibrant green leaves told her it was morning. The shock of her surroundings hit like a splash of ice water. She wasn't in her bed. Her eyes opened wide, and she saw she was laying on sandy ground. Panic rose through her body in a wave of rippling tension. She couldn't hear any human sounds. She couldn't hear any engines or anything electrical. All she could hear was the pure natural sounds of a light breeze through trees, and waves crashing onto a beach close by. She could also hear her own rapid breathing and the beginnings of panicked whimpers escaping from her throat.

The night before, she fell asleep in her apartment, in her own bed. She always slept in the nude, but she woke dressed in shorts and a plain t-shirt. When she went to sleep, winter was already coming on, the ground covered in ice and snow. Each day saw only a few hours of daylight. In just over two months the residents of her Northern Canadian town would not truly see the sun for about a month.

Looking around, the plants were obviously tropical and the air was comfortably warm.

She stood up, pulling the strap of her duffel bag with her. It was a duffel bag she had stored in a closet. But it was here somehow and it was filled. She sat back down with the duffel bag in front of her and squeezed her eyes shut. This had to be a dream. People don't go to sleep in one place and wake up on the other side of the world. The buzzing of insects around her head brought her attention back to the unreality she was experiencing. When she opened her eyes, everything was the same as when she woke up. She swatted at the flying insects, irritated to be bothered by them. She stood up again resolving to figure out this dream or what was really happening.

Looking to her right, the vegetation grew thicker, blocking the sunlight. To her left she saw thinner vegetation, more light and the sound of crashing waves from that direction. She took a step toward the sound of the crashing surf. Fear coursed through her body in waves larger than the waves so clearly heard nearby. She was afraid to leave the spot she woke up in, and afraid to stay there at the same time. She swallowed against the fear induced dryness in her mouth and throat. She took another trembling step, letting her hand reach forward to touch a bare branch in front of her.

The breeze cooled the unnoticed tears on her cheek. The trees resolved into a trail before her. The sandy ground clear of anything growing clearly showed her the path, but she had no idea where it would lead. Stems and leaves pushed easily out of her way as she walked toward the unknown destination.

After a few yards, the palm trees and tropical shrubs cleared enough for her to see the first glimpses of water. Despite her fear pushing her to run back and find her way back home, she continued forward. Somehow she knew she couldn't return home by returning to the place where she woke up.

As she drew closer, she noticed the water was a brilliant shade of liquid crystal blue, with gentle waves cascading onto a sandy beach. She didn't see any human footprints in the sand. There were small tracks across the sand, and ripples caused by the rising and falling tides, but there were no indications any humans were here.

Noticing this caused the lump of fear to rise up in her throat again. It was just so unreal. The breeze brushing against her skin and clothes felt so real. The insects buzzing around her were so real. Even the smell of the salt water was completely real and natural. It just couldn't be possible though. This place had to be thousands of miles from where she fell asleep the night before. She would have had to been on one of the world's fastest aircraft to travel so far in just a few hours and she would have known if she had been on an airplane.

She sat roughly on the sandy ground as the strength left her legs. She sat staring at the ocean in front of her as tears streaked down her face. She felt so overwhelmed that she did not even notice the tears except when they caused her vision to blur.

No matter how long she sat there crying, nothing changed. The waves continued to roll in and crash against the sandy surf. The insects kept buzzing around her. The tears continued to streak down her cheeks, but eventually they slowed and came to a stop as numbness entered her heart. Everything she could cry out was done. She couldn't cry anymore. She didn't move either. For that moment she just sat there and listened to the sounds of the buzzing insects, the crashing waves, and birdcalls from the trees behind her. At times those sounds were quieter and she could hear the sound of her own breathing.

It was the sound of her breathing that got her attention. That sound reminded her that she was alive. She may not have any idea what was happening, but she was alive and she was thirsty.

She used her t-shirt to wipe the tears from her eyes and cheeks. The shirt was noticeably damp from her crying and she could feel the breeze cooling her skin under the fabric. It didn't matter if this was a dream or if it was real, she needed to find something to drink.

She stood up, picking up the duffle bag as she did and looked up and down the beach. To her left the beach stretched on and curved back until she could only see the ocean. To her right, perhaps a couple hundred yards away was an outcrop of rocks that jutted out into the crashing waves. Those rocks were the only thing that looked different. With the duffel bag adjusted on her shoulder, she began walking towards the rocks.

The sand gave way beneath her feet with each step. This would be a perfect secluded beach if she had chosen to come here. Right now it was a scary beach that she wasn't supposed to be on. This beautiful place should have been a dream vacation come true, not a nightmare to be endured. She should have been in a bikini laying on the sand enjoying the sun. Instead she was walking on unsteady feet hoping to find fresh water.

Each step brought the rocks closer, yet they didn't seem to grow closer. She kept walking, placing one unsteady foot in front of the other, knowing that she was moving closer to those rocks that jutted out into the ocean, despite what her eyes tried to tell her. The hardest part of each step was not knowing. Having no idea of whether or not she could find something to drink up ahead. Having no idea of why she was here. Having no idea what she was even supposed to do.

She walked with the tropical trees and brush to her right, staying close to the forest instead of moving further out onto the sandy beach. To her left, the waves crashed against the surf with regularity. The beach was easily large enough for people to be out playing games, enjoying the sunshine and spending time in the ocean. If only there were people here to enjoy it, then maybe this wouldn't feel so much like a nightmare.

As she walked, she thought about home. She thought about her small but cozy apartment where her

neighbor liked to hang things from the nearby balco
Sometimes those things were neat, and sometimes th
made noise in the middle of the night. Like the Halloween skeleton that keep bumping against the wall. She knew the woman was seeing two different men and neither of the men were aware of the other. Maybe that would change soon, but for now she got to play her games.

She thought about the things inside of her apartment, such as the collection of books that were her pride and joy. The lives of people she followed through those pages. The furniture she had worked so hard and painstakingly to find to make the home just right. The right color leather for the couch, the table that was just the right size for her to enjoy presenting meals to friends and family. It seemed she had very few guests since her children moved out, but she did entertain guests sometimes and that table was just perfect for relaxing, talking and enjoying a good meal.

Looking up, she could see she was closer to the rocks. They still seemed further away than she first guessed, but at least she could tell she was getting closer. She didn't think about what it would be like to get there and not find any water. For the moment, she just focused on the first goal of walking to those rocks. Then she would go onto the next goal, whatever that goal would be.

As she arrived at the rocky outcrop, her legs felt tired and rubbery from walking on sand. She felt relieved to set foot on the solid rock. Waves crashed against the rocks to her left. She moved up onto the rocks to get a better view. The outcropping stretched out before her, then dipped down to form a pool of seawater before rising up again. Waves moved sluggishly over rocks out away from the beach, causing the pool to rise and lower as the water moved back and forth. The rocks rose higher to her right. They were rough, but easy to climb. The footing was secure, so she moved higher up on the rocks to improve her view.

She climbed easily up to the level of the top of the trees. Back from the way she came was a jungle. The foliage blocked her from possibly seeing anything useful. The ocean stretched out away from the beach. She could see nothing breaking the expanse of water.

To her right she looked up at a mountain majestically overlooking the beach. The rocky outcrop she stood on was right at the foot of that mountain. The land curved inward, forming a sheer cliff. She couldn't see the bottom of the cliff, but she could see a waterfall cascading off the cliff. Her best guess on the distance was that the waterfall was more than a mile away, and there was no way she was going to be able to walk there from this point. The rocks grew steeper as they went up the mountain, and as they moved further along the beach they grew rougher. From here she wasn't sure she could make it past the first pool.

She felt relieved seeing the waterfall. There was water here, she just needed to find it and soon. She looked back down and saw that the jungle ended before the outcrop. Where it ended, she saw what appeared to be a path that headed inland. Following that path looked like a much better idea than trying to climb the side of the mountain. She climbed down the rocks carefully to reach the path. The ground was firm, a much needed relief after walking on the sand for so long.

The path inland was easy to follow. The jungle to her right, and a rocky wall to her left, the ground remained clear in front of her. The occasional tree, root, or vine on the path was easy to step over as she walked inland. The sound of the waves breaking slowly grew muted behind her while the sounds of insects buzzing around her seemed to grow louder. It was as if they sensed her and came out of the jungle to explore the strange creature invading their territory.

The wall to her left grew broken at points, resolving into a rocky slope with scattered plants. The path before her remained clear though, so she continued to forward. She had no idea where the path led, just as she had no idea where she was or how she came to be here. The sound of breaking waves behind her grew so muted she no longer truly heard them.

She came upon some flat rocks in a shady area. It was hard to judge the position of the sun because of the canopy of trees on her right, but she was pretty sure several hours had passed since she woke up in this place. She paused a moment, realizing she had been walking since she woke up. Her legs were tired and sore from the exertion, so she sat down on one of the rocks with her feet resting on the ground. Leaning forward, she closed her eyes and rested.

The sounds around her became clear as she sat there with her eyes closed. There were so many quiet sounds that all she had to do was listen and she could pick them out; the breeze through the canopy of trees rustling the leaves, the muted breaking waves, water burbling over rocks, insects buzzing nearby, and birds chirping within the forest. Those sounds around her were serene and relaxing. If this was a dream, then it was a nice dream. Who doesn't dream of getting away from everything and being in a place with no other people are around? It was easy to imagine waking up refreshed from a dream like this. Nothing changed though. She could try to imagine this was a dream, but too many instincts told her it wasn't.

It was nice to rest here, but it wasn't solving her current problem. If she really was out in the middle of nowhere, then she needed to find water. After that she could work on the tasks of finding food and shelter, but the first thing she needed was water.

She stood up and adjusted the strap over her shoulder and sighed. The trail ahead went under the canopy of trees, leaving it shrouded in darker shadows than the trail up to this point. Here the rocks pushed the trail right against the edge of the forest, creating a clear area along the trail. The calls of the birds quieted as she looked at the trail, leaving the sound of the breeze, the waves, and the burbling water clearer to her ears.

She realized what she was hearing just as her foot left the ground to take the next step. The action momentarily took away her balance and she almost fell back onto the rocks before she regained it. The pounding in her heart and her own rapid breathing made it difficult to make out the sounds again. She had to force herself to stop breathing for a moment to hear it.

She stood up on the rock and looked around as she listened. As quietly as possible she moved from one rock to another and listened. The sound grew stronger as she crossed the rocks, moving closer to the steep slope of the mountain.

There, she spotted it, a stream of crystal clear water inside a crevice cascading down the side of the mountain. She didn't hear the fall because of the water formed crevice. Where the fall exited the crevice, it formed a pool within the rocks she was on before it fell over the side of the rocks, creating the burbling sound she heard The stream flowed away from the beach, going under brush and trees and out of sight.

She didn't give the destination another thought as she pressed her face into the water and sucked in a delicious mouthful. She pulled back up and delighted in the sensation of water dripping down into her shirt. For the moment all thoughts were out of her mind, all that was left was how wonderful it felt to have her first drink of the day. She drank until she could feel the water sloshing around in her otherwise empty stomach.

She sat on her knees with the jungle to her back. She stared at the crevice the water flowed through for a moment. Then her eyes scanned the wall of the mountain in front of her. It appeared as mostly solid rock with the occasional plant growing on its steep slope. From this angle, she couldn't see more than a few yards up the face before it met the skyline, leaving the bulk of the mountain above hidden from view.

To her left, two trees created a deep shadow against the face. She couldn't even see the rocky wall within the shadow. There wasn't anything about the wall which explained what was happening. At home, the first snowfalls were covering the ground. Each day she could expect about seven hours of real daylight, followed by long nights that would get longer for the next two months before the Winter Solstice.

This place probably did not know what snow was. The plants were clearly tropical. The temperature was definitely warm enough for her to be comfortable wearing shorts and a light t-shirt.

It didn't make any sense. She still could not understand how she could go from falling asleep in her own bed to waking up here. This had to be thousands of miles away from home. What was this place? Was she on a large island or was she on a coast? Being on a coast would mean that people couldn't be too far away. If this was an island, then she would have to hope there were people and she wasn't stranded here alone.

She shuddered as that thought crossed her mind. The idea that she was stranded here alone was the scariest thing she could imagine right now. With an effort she pushed that thought from her mind. Her friends and family would notice she was missing. At some point there would at least be a boat or a plane. She would find a way to let someone know she was here and find a way to get back home.

She slipped the shoulder strap over her head and turned around so she was sitting on her butt instead of her knees. Ahead she could see the jungle grow dense, until there were only spots of sunlight filtering through to the undergrowth.

If she was reading the sun right, it was past noon. If she woke at her normal time, then that would mean she had been wandering around in this jungle for about six hours. How could this be real? About twenty four hours ago she was on her lunch break at work, or maybe she had returned to her desk to finish the paper she was working on yesterday. Today she was going to go over that paper and make sure it was ready to pass on to her boss. Instead she spent her day just searching for water. At least she could say she completed that task successfully. All she needed was someone to say it to.

The duffel bag she had carried since this morning was full. It was yet another mystery in a long line of mysteries. She knew for certain this duffel bag was supposed to be stored away in her hall closet. She used it when she was taking kickboxing classes and put it away when she just didn't have the time to keep going to that class.

She unzipped it slowly, wary of what she would find inside. Sitting on top were two t-shirts and two pair of shorts. The shorts were supposed to be in a storage box until next summer. The t-shirts were supposed to be in her t-shirt drawer. She pulled them out of the duffel bag and set them aside. Below the clothes she found two pocket knives, a large hunting knife, a small first aid kit, flint and steel, a plastic bag with fishing line and hooks, a towel, washcloth, a belt, her black bikini, and a light blanket.

Looking at it all, she couldn't see how it all possibly fit inside the duffle bag. She couldn't understand why she had this survival gear. Something was telling her that she was supposed to be here, and that she was going to need these things to survive. For the moment she could only stare at the items she pulled out of her duffel bag.

She felt numb inside just looking at her things. She couldn't think about what it meant. The thought that she wouldn't be able to just go home tried to invade her thoughts, but somehow it couldn't penetrate the numbness she felt.

A breeze rustled through the leaves and some birds sang out in the forest without her noticing as she sat on the rocks.

Frustrated, she stood and walked about the rocks. This was not making any sense and she needed something to make sense. She needed to know where she was and why she was here, and why she had a duffel bag filled with her clothes and survival items. She paced until she couldn't take it anymore and screamed out her frustration. The birds went quiet, but otherwise nothing responded to her scream. Screaming did not make her feel better, in fact it was the opposite, it made her head hurt. She slowed her pace and focused on her breathing. It was a simple exercise and it worked. She practiced often enough that she could usually get her mind and body to relax when she needed to. It didn't make her feel less upset, but she did feel calm.

She turned slowly as she continued to make her breathing remain calm. When she stopped pacing, she was closer to the shadows she had seen against the wall before and something about the shadows was wrong. They weren't shadows, it was an opening of some sort.

Curiosity pushed her feet to walk closer. She could tell now that it was an opening about as wide as her outstretched arms, and just slightly taller than she. Each step revealed more details, until she could see into the cave. It was a cave, deep enough that she couldn't see the backside of it from outside.

She moved slowly, ready to run if something was inside the cave. She poked her head inside. Her eyes adjusted and she saw the back wall of the cave was just a few feet in. The bottom was covered with sand and broken rocks, and the cave was otherwise empty. The only sign of life were some old webs near the back.

Still uncertain, Michelle stepped into the cave. Once her eyes were adjusted, the sunlight from outside kept the cave well lit. The floor was relatively flat, the walls seemed solid, but cracked stone and the roof looked the same stone as the walls. It was dry and she couldn't smell any animal scents or mustiness inside.

As long as there wasn't something already living here, this would be perfect for shelter. She stayed inside looking over everything in the cave. She could clear enough rocks out of the way to form a decent enough sleeping spot. She felt like she had to duck since the roof was just a couple inches over her head, but for a secure shelter, this was better than anything she could try to make on her own.

Without further hesitation she gathered her things and moved them into the cave. As she moved in, she still couldn't see how all these things fit into her small duffel bag.

When she emerged from the cave after clearing a sleeping space and putting her blanket down on the sand it was near evening. Birds and insects she couldn't see made the jungle alive with sound. The rumbling in her stomach reminded her that she had not eaten anything. The sun was below the level of the top of the trees. True sundown was probably several hours away.

Fear of being in the jungle with the sun going down won out over her stomach. She stayed near the cave, hoping in the morning she would wake up in her own bed.

Sunlight lit up the cave the next morning. She woke tired and sore. Every noise she heard shocked her awake, leaving her certain she had stolen an animals' cave and it was returning to reclaim its territory.

The blanket was bundled up around her, evidence of the tossing and turning she did through the night. Tired or not, she wasn't going to be able to go back to sleep. Wishing she would wake up in her bed didn't happen. Wishing she could just go to her kitchen and get something to eat wasn't going to happen either.

She got up and found a clear area off the trail to relieve herself. Drank enough water to convince her stomach it wasn't completely empty and sat down to think about what to do. There really wasn't much to think about. She needed to find something to eat. Did she go back to the beach, or follow the path that led her to this cave? She didn't remember seeing anything during her walk along the beach, or along the path up to the cave.

She had fishing line, but her only fishing experience was on the lake near her home. She had no idea how to use the fishing line on a beach. That idea was going to have to wait until she felt sure she could take the time to figure out what she needed to do.

She didn't know what she might find in the jungle, but that seemed like the best option. She went back into the cave to get her belt and hunting knife. She knew she didn't really know how to use a knife to defend herself, but she felt better knowing she had it with her.

The trail started off with trees on both sides. The stream of water created a place where they could grow next to the mountain. A few yards along the trail she crossed the stream, but continued following the trail with the mountain on her left. She scanned the plants carefully as she walked, looking for anything that looked edible. She didn't see anything but trees and broad leafy undergrowth. Undaunted, she continued.

Minutes later she encountered a fork in the trail. To the left the trail continued along the side of the mountain. To the right it broke off into an area where the vegetation became less dense. It was still an easy to follow trail, so she took the chance and followed the trail that headed away from the mountain. She looked back behind her so she would know what it would look like on her way back.

She still had jungle on her right, but on her left were broad bladed grasses and some stalk like plants she didn't recognize. The mountain grew more visible as she walked, but she couldn't tell if she could see the top of it or not yet. Beyond the grass on her left, she caught occasional glimpses of more jungle. Then ahead she saw what looked like fruit hanging from a tree.

Elated, she walked faster. The fruit looked like mangos. She didn't see any easily in reach, so she climbed up the trunk of the tree until one of the yellow fruit was just in reach. She sat on a branch with her feet hanging down and bit into the soft flesh and felt the juice of the mango fill her mouth and run down her chin. She didn't care if it got all over her shirt. She was so hungry she quickly devoured the fruit.

She leaned back against the rough bark and enjoyed the feeling of having eaten. She felt momentarily relaxed. The mango was large, but she still ate all of it. Despite the feeling of satisfaction, she climbed higher into the tree to reach for another one of the fruit. She decided next time she would bring her duffel bag so she could carry more.

Through the branches of the tree she saw another tree with red fruit. Excitedly she picked another mango and climbed down to go see what was on the other tree. The fruit was either plums or cherries. She couldn't tell for sure from the ground. The lower branches didn't have any fruit on them as if something or someone had been through and picked the fruit from those branches. She set the mango down and easily climbed up to a higher branch where she could reach the red fruit. She was sure they were cherries, and if something was eating them, then they were probably safe to eat. She popped the first one into her mouth and discovered they were very sweet, and absolutely delicious.

She climbed back to the ground to reclaim her mango and looked around with a satisfied smile on her face. The smile almost faltered as she spotted more fruit trees. The luck of finding this place left her stunned.

She almost ran to the next tree, but stopped herself. She turned around until she spotted the mango tree and remembered her thought about bringing her duffel bag. The thought spurred her back down to the trail to get that duffel so she could gather some fruit.

Before the sun reached its zenith, she returned to the cave with a small assortment of fruits she was familiar with. She spotted several trees in that grove with fruit she didn't recognize. She didn't feel the least bit bothered to try new fruits, but she wasn't sure how to make sure they were safe to eat.

Looking at the cave filled her with a feeling of trepidation. Finding something to eat should have been satisfying, but it reinforced the reality that she was not home. It reinforced that she didn't know what she was going to do to be able to return home. She knew some basic survival skills and she knew she would need to make a signal of some sort so that rescuers could find her. How would they know to even look here though? How would anyone know she was thousands of miles away from home and that she appeared here in less than ten hours?

Somehow she pushed against the depressing thoughts. They were not going to change the reality of her situation and they were not going to help her get back home. She set the fruit down and took a moment to focus on her breathing again. Forcing herself to remain calm and to think through what she needed to do.

That last thought gave her pause. Think. She needed to take the time to think. She could handle this if she would just think first. With that in mind, she closed her eyes and forced herself to breath deeper and slower. Calmness seeped through her slowly, but with surety. It was a start, but she needed more than a start. She stepped outside of the cave and looked at her surroundings. She listened to them. It was the same dense jungle of trees in front of her, the wall of a mountain behind her, a trail that went back to a beach in one direction, a grove of fruit trees and other unknown destinations in the other direction. Birds called out to each other from their unseen perches and nests, insects buzzed among the trees, and waves crashed on the beach.

Slowly but deliberately, she sat down on the flat rock under her feet. It was more than large enough to sit on comfortably. She sat with her legs crossed in the lotus position, closed her eyes and extended her arms out to her sides, palms up. The energy gathered within her, she focused on her breathing and holding her arms at her side. With a slow exhale, she brought her arms up over her head, letting her palms meet directly over her. With the inhale she brought her hand down to the level of her chest, focusing on the negative energy gathered within her body.

On the next exhale she pushed that energy out of her body as she pushed her hands down and away from her body as the palms separated and went back to each side. She let go of everything, releasing all of her fear in the movements of her body and the quieting of her mind. It was not a simple process. She performed these yoga movements at least once a week. When work was stressful they served to bring her relaxation so she could enjoy the comfort of her own home. When people were being difficult, she could push them out of her mind.

Though she had never faced anything as difficult as coming to grips with a reality that should not have been the least bit possible, the practiced yoga movements still brought a calmness to her mind that allowed her to think.

The circumstance required survival. Survival required that she meet her basic needs for water, food, and shelter. She had water. She could hear it burbling over rocks behind her. She had shelter. Her duffel bag and the collected fruits were behind her. She had a source of food from the grove of fruit trees she found this morning. Those trees would not be enough though. The fruit would give her sustenance, but she would need a variety of foods to get the protein, vitamins, and minerals that her body would need. She needed to find a source of meat or at least protein based plants. Two of the three things she needed to survive were already taken care of. Now she needed to focus on the third item and find more sources of food.

The sun was still almost directly overhead. That meant she had time today to explore for other sources of food. There were aboriginal tribes where she lived who still survived on diets almost exclusively of fish. If they could survive on fish, then she could survive on fish. She need only to teach herself to catch them and cook them.

Cooking them would require a fire. That reminded her of the flint and steel she found in her duffel. Whatever mysterious force had brought her here, had at least provided her with a means to survive.

Michelle opened her eyes, the jungle still before her. It did not provide any clues for finding any other food. That was no longer a concern. The jungle was simply a jungle, it wasn't here to give her what she needed. It was here to take what it needed for its own survival.

She chose first to try to understand how to catch fish, but without the expectation that she would succeed today. The small fishing kit sat where she left it beside the duffel bag. Inside of the fishing kit she found a coil of heavy fishing line with six hooks and six lures. It would have been nice to have a fishing pole and a full tackle box, but once again this wasn't something she could concern herself with. This was what she had.

She recalled the beach from the day before. The waves crashing onto the sandy beach and onto the rocks that extended out into the ocean. Trying to cast this line out while standing on the sand would be useless unless she could walk out into the water far enough, and the fish were willing to actually come up to her. Although a pleasant thought, it sounded absurd to her mind. That left the rocks and the hope that she could go out far enough on the rocks to drop a line in the water without risking falling in. She had heard more than enough stories of people who were crushed against rocks after falling into a large lake or ocean.

Carefully she put the line, hooks, and lures back into the plastic bag she had pulled them from. She would explore the beach first and look for safe places from where she could cast out the fishing line. With luck she would spot fish in the water so she would know where to try and catch them.

> You can get addicted to a certain kind of sadness
> Like resignation to the end
> Always the end
> So when we found that we could not make sense
> Well you said that we would still be friends
> But I'll admit that I was glad that it was over
> - Somebody That I Used to Know by Gotye

Michelle walked back along the trail toward the beach. She couldn't recall how far she had walked until she found the stream of water and the cave, but she felt certain it was not too far because she could still hear the sound of crashing waves from the beach.

The trail looked so different in this direction. She knew she was seeing the same features, just from a different perspective, but one change of perspective can make a significant difference. At one point she saw what looked like a trail going diagonally up the wall of the mountain. She noted it so she could explore up there later.

She continued on the trail and within moments received her second largest shock since discovering she was in this strange place. She saw a man on the trail heading toward her. He spotted her and stopped on the trail a few feet in front of her. For the moment she could only stare. He was stopped and staring back at her. His wavy light brown hair was down to his shoulders. He didn't have a shirt on, exposing his sun darkened arms and chest. Blue jean shorts covered his waist and the tops of his legs. She couldn't stand her staring at him wide eyed. She needed help if she was going to get back home.

"Excuse me," She broke the silence between them. As she spoke, the words came out faster. "I need help. I don't know where I am. I don't know how I got here. I need help finding food, and I need help so I can go back home."

Saying the word home brought a lump to her throat. She had to pause and take a breath, knowing that if she tried to continue she would cry. He stood there, staring at her. She saw that he had a fish speared and held over his shoulder. His only movement was his chest rising and falling with his breath. She couldn't tell if he even understood what she said.

"Parlez-vous Francáis? S'il vous plait, j'ai besoin d'aide." She spoke in French, the only other language she knew.

"I don't speak French!" His voice was deep, somewhat rough. It was like he was irritated that she had spoken French.

"Oh thank God. I was afraid you didn't understand me. I woke up in the jungle yesterday. I don't know how I got here, but I want to go home." Relieved to hear him speak.

"I can't help you." His voice was still gruff.

Those words left her stunned to tears. How could he not try to help someone he didn't know? Couldn't he see she was desperate? She couldn't swallow the lump in her throat, or keep the fear out of her voice. "Please?" She continued, "I really need help. I don't know what to do."

"I didn't say won't help. I said can't help." He stated.

A tear rolled down her cheek. She almost didn't understand what he was saying, but somehow it did get through. She looked at him carefully. The wavy hair down to his shoulders had a slightly unkempt look The shorts were faded and frayed around the waist and the bottom edges. The fish was impaled on a sharpened stick, something he could have easily made from one of the trees or stalks from the jungle. He looked like he lived here. Could it be that he woke up here one morning just like she did?

"Even if I could help you, I doubt either one of us could think of a reason why I would want to help."

"What do you mean?" Despite the tears on her cheeks, she couldn't mask the irritation she felt that anyone would say such a thing.

"You apparently don't recognize me. I know you. I don't like you." He answered with the same irritated gruff tone of voice. He meant what he said. How could he know her though? How could anyone know who she was when she wasn't anywhere close to home?

She looked at him again, looked at his face. The green eyes looked back at her. Those eyes were cold though, reflecting the truth of his words that he did not like her. She recognized him. The last time she saw him, his hair was cut short and he was at least thirty pounds heavier. It wasn't just the weight lost though. He was in better shape. The definition of the muscles in his arms, chest and stomach was clearly evident. The man she remembered belonged in an office; the man before her belonged in this jungle.

The voice was the same though. She recognized that anger and bitterness now. The same voice she heard so many times before she finally stopped talking to him and blocked him from having any contact with her. She remembered the relief she felt getting him out of her life. He refused to understand that she did what she had to do for herself. Between work and trying to find a place to live, she couldn't be there for him the way he wanted, expected, or possibly the way he needed. She had to stop talking to him to take care of herself, but his resentment just never ceased. In the end there was no choice but to just cut him off completely.

He didn't understand. Clearly he would never understand. She felt like everything dropped inside of her. Waking up to this strange place seemed like the worst thing she could imagine. That thought was wrong though, things clearly got worse.

"Frank, that was a long time ago. Can't you just get over it already?" Michelle asked with exasperation and irritation.

Frank responded by pulling out a hunting knife like the one she wore at her waist. Light glinted off the blade as he looked around for a moment before spotting what he was looking for. With an easy, deft move, he stabbed the blade into a tree, taking a chunk out of the side of it with the sturdy blade.

Fear kept Michelle rooted to the spot as she watched. It subsided only a small amount as he returned the knife to its sheath. "Tell the tree to get over it, and when it does you can come tell me to just get over it too!" The anger and animosity in his voice left no room for doubt about his feelings.

Anger overcame her, fueled by fear and so much pain from the past, "You know what Frank? This is stupid. I only asked for help, and now you're taking it out on trees too. Have you become so pathetic you can't even help someone in need?"

His eyes seemed even colder as that piercing green gaze turned on her. "Go back to where you came from Michelle. Get out of my life and stay the hell out of it this time. You aren't getting anything else from me ever!" With that final exclamation he pushed past her, barely avoiding touching her as he did.

Fear kept Michelle speechless until he was past. Then she realized she couldn't think of anything to say. She was stuck in the middle of nowhere and the only person she saw hated her. He turned and headed up the trail she had just passed. She didn't like the idea of exploring up there now. Part of her wanted to yell at him. To get that last word in, but what would be the point?

She turned back to the path and her eyes caught on the white scar on the tree Frank stabbed with his knife. Another tear fell down her cheek. "Get over it." She told the tree quietly and turned to walk back to her cave.

> She embraced with a smile
> As she opened the door
> A cold wind blows
> It puts a chill into her heart
> - Restless by Within Temptation

Michelle watched the steady drizzle falling outside her cave. The day started overcast and rainy and did not change. It matched her mood. Frank's words yesterday still rang in her ears. She felt even more helpless today. She felt so lethargic and depressed she could only pick at the fruits she had picked yesterday morning.

She thought about home as she sat there. She missed everything. Even the toilet that she had to rattle the handle before the water would stop running. She wished again that she could have the chance to talk to her son and daughter. They were both close enough to talk to if she just took the time. Both were adults, Aaron had his own apartment and a nice job, while Zoey was away at the University most of the year. She wasn't more than a phone call away, but the last time she called was more than two weeks ago, now it seemed like it was years ago. With Aaron, it was longer though. He dropped by one night before going out with friends, and barely had time to say hi before he was on his way. She didn't even think about not seeing him later and just said hi and wished him a good night before going back to reading her book. She had the chance right then to talk to him, and she missed it, instead just reading a book that didn't matter as much as her son.

The cave remained dry except for when she cried and the tears fell to the sandy ground unnoticed. The rain fell, drenching the leaves and rocks she could see outside, but it didn't reach into where she sat. The air was cooler than the day before, but warm enough she didn't feel uncomfortable sitting in her shorts and t-shirt. The rain continued all day long. It was either a steady drizzle, or fat drops coming down.

The rain changed toward the end of the day though. It had to be too early for sunset, but the sky grew very dark within minutes. The green leaves became wet black shadows outside the cave, and the first bolt of lightning lit up the sky and the jungle. The wind followed, blowing the leaves in a gust that broke some branches inside the forest. Michelle moved back away from the mouth of the cave as more lightning lit up the sky and jungle. The wind grew stronger still, until it was howling outside the mouth of the cave.

When the flashes of lightning faded away, everything became so pitch black Michelle could not see anything except the purple afterimages in her eyes. Each flash of lighting and blast of thunder sent fear shivering through her body. The temperature fell and she pulled her blanket up around her, shielding her from the cooler air and from the frightening storm. It raged for hours as she sat there watching outside the cave. She watched as lightning lit up trees bent with the force of the wind.

The storm eventually blew itself out. The lightning finally slowed down and thunder became muted rumbles in the distance. The cave was left pitch black. So dark she couldn't see her hand even if she brought it up in front of her face. The sound of rain falling steadily filled the cave.

Michelle stayed curled up under the blanket leaning against the rock wall and fell asleep.

Sunlight and the sound of something hitting a tree close to her cave woke Michelle from her restless sleep. Muscles in her neck and back complained and stiffened from trying to sleep against the rock wall. It sounded like someone was trying to chop wood just outside and she was tempted to go tell them to stop so she could go back to sleep. She was tired and sore and just wanted to lay back down and get more rest.

She remembered where she was though. She was still lost in some strange jungle, close to the ocean. She forced her body to move, throwing her blanket back to the sandy spot she would have preferred to sleep on. The action made muscles in her neck twinge with pain. Sleeping against the side of the cave was definitely a bad idea, no matter how bad the storm was.

She got up, brushed sand off her clothes and stepped out of the cave. The sun was well up until it was almost blinding. The sky was a brilliant shade of blue and every color seemed more vibrant. The ground was littered with broken twigs and leaves. Everything was still wet from the storm, but the sun would dry it out soon enough.

The sound of chopping wood was coming from up the trail she would take to get to the grove of fruit trees.

Tentatively she decided to see who or what was making the noise, hoping it wasn't Frank, but sure that was who she would see. She wasn't wrong, just a few feet up the trail she spotted him. His back was to her as he swung what looked like a homemade stone axe against a log laying across the trail.

She watched as he swung one more time and the log split. He was either covered with rain water from the leaves above him, or covered in sweat, or maybe a mix of both, but he was clearly wet. His long hair clung to his skin in dark strands, and water dripped down his back, soaking into the waist band of his jean shorts. Those shorts were already so wet they were clinging to him like a second skin.

She wanted to turn away, but he was the only other person here and for the moment she didn't feel alone. He set the stone axe down, grabbed the freshly cut end of the log, then pushed and lifted. The muscles in his back strained with the effort as he forced the log off the trail, pushing it into brush off to the side.

As he sat down to rest, Michelle turned and walked back to her cave. The memories of the confrontation two days ago remained fresh in her mind. She couldn't face that hatred again. Just facing this place was hard enough, she didn't need someone yelling at her for things years in the past.

Just the thought brought back some of those memories, especially all the horrible things he posted on Facebook. The way he went on and on about the breakup, and the accusations he made still stung. She kept track of him and read what he wrote for a year after breaking up before he cut her off so she couldn't read what he wrote anymore. The cut off came after a failed attempt to be friends.

She tried so hard to be friends with him. The tears she cried when she realized how much her actions had hurt him were real. He didn't seem to understand that though. He was moving on, but still expected she would be there for him. She couldn't do that. She needed to move on and she couldn't do that talking to him every day. Why couldn't he have accepted that? They could have stayed in touch. They could have talked, but just as friends and both of them moving on with their lives.

That was years ago now. It was the same time of year that they broke up as she found herself in this mysterious place. That thought made her pause outside her cave. Was there a connection? Why did bad things connected to Frank happen at this time of year? Was the universe playing some perverse joke on her?

Why would something like this even happen? Michelle knew she was a good person. She didn't treat people badly. She kept to a motto of live and let live. She accepted other people's choices for what they wanted to do with their lives. Why would something like this even happen to her?

She realized she was about to hit the rock wall in front of her and pulled her fist up short. She couldn't afford to injure herself. Just imagining trying to survive with a broken hand sent shivers down her spine and calmed the anger rising in her chest.

She needed to survive. She couldn't allow herself to die here and never see her children again. She couldn't consider not seeing her sister, her parents, or her friends again. Resolved to survive, Michelle pushed Frank out of her mind and assessed what she needed to do. Water and shelter were taken care of. She had one source of food, but she needed more than fruit to survive.

She did her best to ignore the mess left behind by the storm. Two days ago she was going back to the beach to see if she could attempt to catch fish from there. It would also give her a chance to explore the area.

The fishing line and hooks were still in their pouch where she left them. The flint sitting beside the pouch caught her attention, reminding her that she would need to start a fire if she managed to catch something. It would be a good idea to try starting a fire either way, if she could find some dry wood.

With the pouch of fishing line in hand, Michelle walked to the beach stepping over broken branches and walking through fallen leaves that littered the path. The fury of the storm was evident with every step. Raindrops continued to fall from the leaves above, creating a light rainfall underneath the tree branches that left her shirt wet and clinging to her skin.

The sunlight on the beach was a welcome sight when she arrived. She didn't remember walking so far in from the beach to find the cave. She realized that was three days ago.

The noise from the crashing waves filled her ears. She loved beaches, and loved the ocean, but that was when she got to go enjoy them by choice. Here the sound was a horrible reminder that somehow her entire world had been taken away from her, or the better statement was that she had been taken from her world.

Taking a deep calming breath, Michelle surveyed the crashing waves in front of her. They rolled up onto the sand, and rolled back into the ocean. The only chance to catch a fish there would be to wade out into the water and hope the fish swam up to her. To her right she surveyed the rocks jetting out into the water. The tide was lower, exposing rocks she didn't remember seeing the first time she passed by here.

Carefully, she climbed onto the wet rocks and walked out onto them. Mist from the crashing waves coated her skin, but she found a promising spot. Pools formed among the rocks that she could reach with her fishing line. She just needed bait and hopefully she could catch fish right here.

Satisfied with what she found, she turned and went back to the sand. From there she surveyed the jungle. There had to be grubs, worms, or insects somewhere in that green foliage that she could catch for bait. The small buzzing gnats seem to be present around her at all times until now she barely noticed them.

She stepped to the brush, picking her way in carefully. She didn't want to let the beach get out of her sight. This area did not have any trails, and she wasn't going to go crawling among the trees and get lost. The ground, though sandy, was solid enough for the plants to grow here, but she didn't see anything that looked like fish bait.

Undaunted she continued her search. Walking over fallen leaves and twice stepping over trees knocked down by the storm. She was sure her search lasted over an hour when she decided she wasn't getting anywhere searching along the beach. The warmth from the sun, and the humidity from the evaporating rainwater left her skin feeling sticky and uncomfortable.

The trip back up the trail toward her cave seemed faster than the trip to the beach. Water still dripped from the leaves, but it was much less than when she first passed through.

Frank wasn't anywhere in sight when she got back to her cave. She couldn't hear anything indicating he was nearby. A grumbling in her stomach interrupted her thoughts and reminded her she had not eaten yet. She didn't have any fruit remaining in her cave, thus her only choice was to go back to the grove of fruit trees.

The sight of wood chips on the trail reminded her that she needed to build a fire. It was a task she had put off long enough. The log Frank had pushed off the trail was still there where he pushed it. She would need wood for a fire, so there was no sense letting it go to waste.

Michelle bent down and wrapped her hands and arms around the log, pulled, and it barely moved. "What the hell?" She exclaimed with a surprised exhale. How freaking heavy was this log? She clearly remembered watching Frank pick it up and push it off the trail. It couldn't be that heavy, but she couldn't pick it up. Frustrated, she bent down to try again. She felt her muscles strain with the effort, but the log still barely moved.

He was strong. She knew he was stronger, he was a man after all, but she always felt like he wasn't that much stronger. He was though. He was far stronger than she was, and he wasn't going to help her.

With that thought ringing through her mind, Michelle got up and walked quickly along the trail to the grove. She passed two more cut logs along the trail, and each one made her angrier as she walked. When she reached the grove, she saw the ground was littered with fallen fruit. Far more than she could possibly eat, but it was more than enough for now.

She picked among the fruits and selected a large pear like fruit. She sat down to eat and as she did her emotions calmed down. She knew that Frank was not being fair, but she couldn't do anything about it. Whatever he was still so upset about was his problem. Her problem was just making sure she survived being stuck here.

The core of the pear struck a branch as she threw it out to the grassy area. At least the grumbling in her stomach had stopped, but she still felt hungry. Resigned to eating fruit, she gathered several, cradled in her shirt, and walked back to her cave.

As she passed by the wood chips on the trail, Michelle decided to put a fire together before sundown. She knew just how dark it could get now, and she didn't want to face another night unable to see anything.

She knew how to build a fire, but she had not had an opportunity to build one from scratch in years. Her memories told her it wouldn't be easy, but it could be done. The hardest task would be finding dry wood and tinder. The storm left everything soaked. The vegetation she could see was all green and growing, definitely not the material she needed to build a fire.

An hour later, she had a stack of broken twigs and branches outside of her cave. It was all green, or wet. Despite getting off the trail and searching the underbrush, she didn't find any wood that was dry enough to start a fire with. She spread out what she had on the rocks where the sun could dry it faster, and began shaving strips from larger sticks to start the fire with. Luckily the knife was good and sharp and she was able to cut the strips without too much difficulty. Starting a fire would have been way easier if she had matches to work with, but instead she had to get stuck here with flint and steel.

      She took a break to get something to drink and wipe the sweat away from her brow when the sun was well past its zenith. Refreshed, she turned her attention to starting the fire. Despite her best efforts though, the kindling was too wet to start a fire with. Every spark that hit it died before it had a chance to catch. The day faded to dusk on the small circle of rocks she set up outside her cave. Mentally she thanked whatever allowed her to find the cave in the first place and that had a nice flat area in front of it. The fire wouldn't be protected from a storm if another blew in, that was something she knew she would have to try and fix later.

> It's a quarter after one
> I'm all alone
> And I need you now
> Said I wouldn't call
> But I've lost all control
> And I need you now
> - Need You Now by Lady Antebellum

Dawn shined bright again. The dew on the rocks outside the cave was already drying when she stepped out of her cave. The wood and kindling she collected were sitting inside the cave just in case it had rained during the night. If the sun came out like it did yesterday, she would lay them out so the sun could dry them out.

Frustration burned brightly in her. She needed a fire, and she needed food and for some reason she just couldn't seem to make either one of them happen. Hunger pains gnawed at her stomach despite eating a few bites of fruit. It just wasn't enough.

Her head hurt from the frustration and lack of sleep. The comfortable bed in her apartment was at least a thousand miles away and it might as well have been a million for all that mattered right now. None of that mattered right now. Wishing she was home didn't make the headache go away and it didn't make her stomach stop growling for real food or something to drink other than water.

Going over those thoughts was not going to find bait for fishing, or find any other source of food. She walked from the cave and looked around hoping to see something she could use as bait. Nothing appeared. There wasn't anything to be found at the beach, so she tried the other direction, heading toward the grove, maybe she could find something among the fruit.

The log Frank chopped through yesterday rested where he left it. She didn't like seeing it there, reminding her that he was strong enough to take care of it and she wasn't. While staring at the log, paused on the trail, she almost missed the bug crawling across it. But she did see it. That was what she needed.

Without hesitation she reached out and grabbed the fat bug only to realize she didn't have anything to hold it in except for her hand. Excited she raced back to the cave to get her fishing kit and then back to the beach before she could lose her only bait.

Looking back she thanked the Universe that she knew how to tie the hook to the line and put the bug on the hook. She lived in a lakeside town and had done her share of fishing in that huge lake. In minutes the baited hook was in the water ready for a fish to come and take the bait.

Despite patiently waiting and hoping for two hours, she not only did not catch a fish, but the water moving back and forth pulled her bait off the hook. With a sigh she pulled the line from the water and went back to her cave. The shavings sat just inside the cave where she left them, still damp from the previous rain.

Hungry and hurting, she sat on the rocks outside her cave. As her head hung down, the first teardrop hit the ground between her legs. She pulled her knees up and held them as the tears formed and fell. Each tear marked a measure of defeat. She couldn't find anything to eat other than the fruit trees. She couldn't catch a fish, she couldn't start a fire. Why was she here? Why was this happening? Her shoulders shook as sobs racked her body.

In that moment she knew she needed help. She couldn't survive like this. The tears poured harder as she forced herself to admit she had only one option. Frank. The only choice she had now was to go to him and ask for help. She needed him if she was going to survive.

The sun was well past its zenith when her tears finally subsided. Wearily she went to the spring and washed her face off. She didn't have anything to see her reflection, and hoped she had cleaned up enough to look at least presentable. Mud covered the shirt and shorts she wore. Her only other change of clothes was not in better shape. She could feel dirt and grime weighing on her short hair, and without a shower or bath, she knew she must look a terrible mess.

Without enthusiasm she peeled and ate a citrus fruit. It was similar to an orange, but the flavor was closer to a tangerine. At the moment it hardly mattered, it was just something to keep her stomach from growling so much. It helped some, but throughout her body, she still needed more.

She ran her fingers through her hair as she stood up, hoping she didn't look as bad as she felt. The choice was clear and no matter how much she hated it, she had to go find him and ask for help.

Her eyes barely saw the trail or where her feet fell as she walked. The path up the hill was an easy walk and switched back once about half way up. The sound of human activity reached her ears before she crested the top of the hill. At the top she spotted Frank with his back to her as he sat working on something beside his fire. An impaled fish roasted over the fire. The scent caused fresh grumblings in her stomach and made her mouth water immediately. The sight of the cooking fish captured her attention so thoroughly she didn't even notice Frank was standing and staring at her until he cleared his throat. The sound brought her attention back from the fish and onto Frank. She felt the familiar lump in her throat just looking at him. She realized it wasn't him that caused the lump in her throat, it was the realization that she wasn't alone here, he was a real person and he was here too.

The lump in her throat robbed her of her voice, leaving her capable of only staring at him. He was still wearing cut off shorts and no shirt. His skin was brown from the sun, his wavy brown hair so long it brushed his shoulders. His green eyes looked dispassionate.

"Why are you here?", his question breaking the silence between them.

She covered her mouth as she swallowed against the lump in her throat. A fresh tear drop formed in her eye, causing her vision to blur for a moment. It seemed forever before she could speak, but she did find enough strength to say what she needed to say. "I need help." The sound of her voice was filled with more unshed tears and desperation.

The sound of the crackling fire and breeze through the leaves of bushes nearby filled her ears following her voice. She couldn't even look at him after admitting she had failed to take care of herself. The breeze slowed, the leaves stopped rustling and she heard only the fire. Crying freely she looked up at him. He stood there just staring.

"Frank. Please. I can't do this. I can't find enough to eat, and I can't build a fire. I hate this. I want to go home, but I can't, and I just need help." The words poured out in an emotional rush that she couldn't contain. "I'll do whatever I can to pay you back. Just please help me."

"STOP!" His voice was rough and demanding. "Just stop already Michelle. I already told you I couldn't think of any reason why I would help you."

Her hands came up to cover her ears. She cried harder as she tried to block out the hatred in his voice. The entire world collapsed around her. She heard only the sound of her crying, and closed her eyes against seeing anything. She fell to her knees without any realization of what she was doing. Rocking and back and forth she couldn't find the strength to do anything else but sit there crying. All of the desperation and all of her need meant nothing. How could she go back to trying to survive when she was failing so badly? Why did he hate her so much he couldn't see she needed help?

She felt more than saw something brush her bare legs. Somehow she cleared the tears out of her eyes and saw the fish laying on the ground in front of her knees. It didn't register in her mind why the fish was laying on the ground. She brushed at her eyes with her hands, trying to clear the tears and clear her mind. Frank was still standing over by the fire, just staring at her.

"Just take it and go Michelle. I don't want to see you. My life was fine without you, and I don't want you back." His tone was softer, but still so cold.

With sobs still escaping, she tried to pick up the fish, it was still hot and steaming from cooking. Somehow she managed to get it picked up and cradled in the bottom of her shirt. She couldn't stop crying or even speak as she turned away from Frank's camp and returned to her cave.

Everything inside and out felt numb as she sat in the entrance of her cave eating the fish. She barely tasted any of it, but she ate all that she could pick from the bones. The tears had dried, the screaming in her mind had subsided, leaving her mind mercifully blank and empty. The food sated her stomach for the first time in days, but she didn't care. Empty of thoughts and emotions she crawled to her blanket where she curled up and fell asleep before the sun had set.

> I'm not afraid to cry
> every once in a while even though
> Goin' on with you gone still upsets me
> There are days every now and again
> I pretend I'm okay
> But that's not what gets me
> - What Hurts The Most by Rascal Flatts

The small fire popped as she cracked the shell of a crab. She didn't know how many weeks had passed since she last spoke to Frank. She saw him sometimes, usually in passing. He left her alone and by the same token she left him alone. The shavings she first made eventually dried enough for her to build a fire. She learned the lesson from that storm and kept wood in her cave where it would stay dry and available for her when she needed it.

Fishing was an unlucky prospect in which she lost her bait far more often than she even saw a fish. During one of the days she was out fishing, Frank came out to the beach. He carried a short stick with a sharpened point that he used for a fishing spear. He had a line of thin rope tied to the spear, and she watched as he tied the other end of the rope to his ankle. He stood there patiently for over an hour before he threw the spear. His throw wasn't successful. He stayed undaunted, and after two more attempts he speared a fish and brought it in quickly. His moves were efficient and practiced.

Jealousy coursed through her veins as she watched him, wishing she could get a fish on her own. She waited a few minutes after he left before she left the beach herself.

The crabs were further down the beach where the waves crashed onto the sand. The first time she saw them they scared her. The claws looked huge and menacing as they crawled about the beach. The sight of them left her running back and screaming. When her heartbeat and breathing finally slowed she was able to approach slowly and watch them. There were baby ones and large ones. As she watched, a gull swooped in and captured one of the baby crabs. The mother held her claws up to defend the remaining babies as they crawled to the water.

The gull reminded her that she had eaten crab before. They were a source of food and they were right here, all she had to do was figure out how to get one. She didn't want to mess with one that was defending the babies though. In moments she found a somewhat stout stick and a rock. Then she watched for one that was more or less by itself.

It took three hits from the stick and another from the rock to make it stop moving. By the time she was done her heart was pounding in her chest and she was practically panting. The crab lay at her feet with its shell cracked. She did it. She captured something to eat besides fruit. She managed the first weak smile in weeks. Carefully she carried her prize back to her cave, ignoring the crabs behind her and the gulls overhead. She stoked her fire and enjoyed having real meat that she managed to get on her own. That crab was the first of several until she was sure she didn't want to ever see another crab in her life.

A few times while she observed Frank, she saw him eat the leaves from one of the plants. She kept track of which plant it was and tried it also. The leaves were kind of spicy sweet, easy to chew and swallow. When nothing bad happened, she studied the plant so she could find more and from time to time ate the leaves to supplement her diet.

The storms came without warning, killing her fire and making her nights miserable. She tried putting a fire in the mouth of her cave, but the smoke was as bad as the winds howling outside the cave. She was good at getting a fire going with the flint and steel now that she was getting plenty of practice, but she didn't know how long it was going to last. At some point she knew she would have to find another way to either keep a fire going or to be able to start one.

She searched the skies and the ocean as often as she could. She never saw anything. She didn't see any airplanes and she didn't see any boats. It was like she was in a world where there were no other people but her and Frank. At times she thought about the past with Frank and wondered why things had gone so horribly wrong that even though they were the only two people here, they couldn't talk.

> I'm tired of being what you want me to be
> Feeling so faithless, lost under the surface
> I don't know what you're expecting of me
> Put under the pressure of walking in your shoes
> - Numb by Linkin Park

Michelle stared at the fish roasting over the fire. Willing it to cook faster as her stomach grumbled in anticipation of the food. She had spent the entire day trying to catch this one small fish, and had not eaten anything else. She did not understand how Frank could so easily catch fish. It seemed like every day he went fishing, he came back with enough fish to last a week.

She knew better than to bother asking Frank to share. He clearly still carried a grudge from the end of the relationship. He had made it perfectly clear that he wasn't going to do anything to help her. Which was fine for her, she didn't want any more handouts from a man who couldn't accept her for who she was, and couldn't accept that she did what she needed to do. She didn't want charity from someone who could so easily turn and talk about her so evilly to anyone and everyone.

She could have gone to the grove for fruit, but she needed more than fruit to live on. She didn't know the plants here, which meant she didn't know which of them might be safe to eat except for what she discovered from Frank.

She sat with her back to her cave, the place where she had found shelter the first day. There was a comfortable sandy spot for sleeping, and enough room to store the few things she had in her duffel bag, as well as a few other things she had picked up for survival since she had arrived on this cursed island.

Once cooked she carefully pulled the fish back from the fire. It was so tender it was ready to fall off her stick and into the fire. Steam poured off the white meat as her mouth watered. She burned her fingers as she touched the meat. Quietly muttering to herself as she licked the burned fingers. For a moment she savored the flavor of the fish on her tongue. She had to use all of her willpower to go slow, so she wouldn't burn herself again. She felt so anxious to eat that it seemed forever for the fish to cool enough to eat. Still, she did burn her fingers and tongue slightly, and considered it a small price to pay for something to eat. When it was gone, she wanted more, but that fish was all she had for today. The sun was going down, and she was not going to go out foraging in the dark. She closed her eyes and leaned back against a rock enjoying the feel of the air against her skin, and the slight warmth of the fire.

A knocking sound caught her attention. She opened her eyes, turned her head slightly and saw Frank standing a dozen feet away. He had used a stick to knock on the tree he was standing beside. What in the hell could he possibly want? She hated the fact that she wanted to just look at him, and wanted him to stay away from her at the same time. He was still a good looking man, and clearly his time on this island had been good to him. The weight he had lost and his improved muscle tone looked good and she hated the feeling that she wanted to look at him.

With a mental scowl, she pushed those thoughts out of her mind. So what if she hadn't seen any other man in who knows how long? So what if she missed a man's touch. She wasn't going to give into this man. She wasn't going to let her body betray her. No matter how much she felt that familiar throbbing sensation in the pit of her stomach. She could and would deal with that later.

"Back in World War One soldiers fought in the trenches in Europe." he said.

"What do you want Frank?" Michelle interrupted. Anger clearly marked her words.

"I would like to finish what I was saying without being rudely interrupted." He just looked at her with his green eyes attempting to pierce into her.

She stared back at him, she wasn't going to let him beat her, not even in a staring contest. "Why should I bother to listen to anything you have to say? I already know what you think about me, and I don't care to hear it again."

He just stared at her his expression unchanging. He didn't look angry. It was the same focused look he had the one day she watched him fishing.

"Fine! Whatever. Say what you have to say, and then leave me alone." She knew she was relenting, but she couldn't stand him just standing there staring like that.

"As I was saying, the soldiers in World War One fought in trenches. Those trenches were sometimes close enough that enemy soldiers could have conversations with each other if they had wanted. One night, during a lull in the fighting, the Germans on one side, I think English on the other, a soldier began to sing a Christmas song. He sang because it was Christmas Eve, and on that night, no one was fighting. In moments, other soldiers joined in the song. Then to their surprise, enemy soldiers joined in the song. As the song ended, the two groups of soldiers looked across the battlefield at each other. They laid down their arms, came out of their trenches, to join together in the middle to celebrate Christmas. For that one night, they had a truce. They did not fight, instead they sang together and created one night of peace. Christmas Eve is two nights from tonight. I am calling a truce. You are welcome to join me for dinner on Christmas Eve and Christmas day."

She sat stunned, unable to think or move. It was Christmas. That meant she had been on this island two and a half months. "How do you know it's Christmas?"

He held up his arm and she saw a watch on his wrist. It was clear that whatever survival gear he found with when he woke up on this island included his wrist watch.

He was offering a truce, and she didn't hear anger in his voice. The thoughts about not accepting anything from him crossed her mind again, but the feeling in her stomach of wanting more to eat was there too. She couldn't deny that she wasn't doing well at surviving. It was clear that she had lost weight since arriving on this island. What was worse was the feeling that she had lost some of her strength as well.

"I accept your truce Frank." She said. She could feel a lump beginning to form in her throat as she spoke the words. She looked back at her fire. "I'll join you for Christmas Eve and Christmas day dinner."

She had no idea why she was accepting his offer.

"Good night then." He said and turned to walk away.

She glanced up long enough to see him leaving, then turned back to her fire and her thoughts. Christmas. She hadn't seen her children or her friends in over two months, and now she was going to spend Christmas without them. The lump in her throat finished forming, and tears rolled down her cheeks unhindered.

She felt so alone. The only other person on the island didn't want anything to do with her. She accepted that and avoided him. She was alone. She pulled her knees up and put her head on them as sobs wracked her body and her strength poured away in her tears.

The fire was nearly out when the sobs stopped shaking her body. Her face and legs were wet from how much she had cried. She threw the remains of her fish into the dying fire and crawled into her cave, undressed and laid on her blanket where loneliness brought fresh tears. She cried until her body fell asleep.

> Where there is desire
> There is gonna be a flame
> Where there is a flame
> Someone's bound to get burned
> Just because it burns
> Doesn't mean you're gonna die
> You've gotta get up and try....
> - Try by Pink

Michelle arrived at the top of the hill where Frank's cave was in the late afternoon. She was sure it was before normal dinnertime, but she didn't have anything else to do but sit at her cave feeling the loneliness again. She felt the need to be near someone, even Frank, for just a little bit.

Frank had his back to her and was chopping something as she arrived. He had a spit set up over his fire and something roasting. It clearly wasn't fish, but where could he have found another source of meat? She didn't look too closely, though she was very tempted to go and see what he was up to and what he had done that she might be able to do herself.

Despite the desires of her stomach, her eyes went back to Frank. He was wearing his jean shorts and sandals, and nothing else. His wavy brown hair was almost down to his shoulders and moved gently in the breeze. She could easily see the muscles in his back and his legs as he worked on whatever he was chopping. For a moment she couldn't tear her eyes away from his sun browned skin and the muscles rippling under that skin. She felt the familiar rush of heat from her loins through her entire body and her fingers tingled as that rush went through her.

With an effort, she clinched her fists and pushed those thoughts away again. She distracted herself wondering how he could stand it. It was clear he had been here longer. He desired sex every bit as much as she did. That was why they were in the relationship together, because they wanted sex so much, and wanted it with each other. But the sex was the biggest thing. They lived so far apart and somehow they both abstained from sex for each other during that relationship. Looking back she wondered how they went so long without sex during that time they were apart. She still felt confused that she gave up sex for him, and that he gave it up for her. It was just their nature to want sex. She unclenched her fists and cleared her throat.

He turned, and smiled. Smiled? At Michelle?

"Hi. I'm glad you didn't change your mind. I have a lot of food here." He said.

"Is there anything I can help with?" She asked as she stepped over to see what he was working on. She almost couldn't contain her surprise when she saw the vegetables he was chopping on a wooden plank. Where did he find those?

She realized he must have noticed the look in her eyes. He had a slightly crooked grin on his face when she looked back at him. That grin gave him an almost boyish look. With the beard and mustache though, he was very clearly a man. Standing this close, she could smell his scent too. He had a cleanliness about him, but she could still smell his musky scent. She felt her groin throb as she inhaled him.

"Could you check on the pork while I finish this up?" he asked.

"Sure." she almost whispered. She could feel the heat in her cheeks, and quickly turned back to the fire. She thought about how she had cried herself to sleep two nights in a row, and now her body was begging her to have the only man in sight. What was she thinking accepting this invitation?

The pork was sitting well above the fire where it would cook slowly. The outside was nice and crispy, but she could clearly see red fluid seeping out in cracks, indicating it needed to cook longer. She turned it on the spit so that it could cook evenly. He had a good bed of hot coals under the pork. She couldn't tell if more wood would be needed or not. For now, she stepped back away from the heat. She already felt hot enough without being that close to the fire.

"Would you like something to snack on while we wait for that to finish cooking?" She heard him asking from behind her.

"That sounds great." She replied honestly. Seeing the pork and the vegetables was making her intensely hungry. The only meat she had eaten since coming to this island was fish or crab. Though both were satisfying, knowing she was going to have something different was really making her mouth water. The pork smelled incredible roasting over the fire like it was.

He handed her what looked like a clay plate with some nuts on it. It was still another treat. She hadn't had any nuts since coming here either. She was going to have to keep her eyes open to find where these nuts were growing. It looked like at least three different kinds of nuts. She picked up a few and put them in her mouth, and tasted the salt first. Her eyes opened in surprise as she tasted the salt before crunching into the nuts.

"Where did you get salt?" The surprise was clearly evident in her voice.

"I filtered and boiled away salt water so that I could collect the sea salt. I had no idea how much water I would have to boil away though. It was worth every bit of effort." He answered.

She didn't say or ask anything else, instead she went back to eating and savoring the salted nuts he had given her.

Once they were gone, she couldn't resist rubbing her finger on the plate and licking off the rest of the salt.

By this time, he had set the vegetables aside. He brought out two crudely made clay cups and poured some water into them from a similarly made pitcher. Without a word he handed one of the cups to her and she very gratefully accepted it. The water and nuts felt good in her stomach, leaving her feeling content for the moment. The roasting pork and fire provided a good distraction to keep her from looking at him.

The need in her body remained persistent and pushed into her thoughts. She pushed back at that need with the memories of how much she hated him. She hated him for the way he acted when their relationship ended and she hated the way he treated her on this island. Yet here she was about to have dinner with him and it seemed like they were old friends getting back together.

He refilled her cup without being asked, then poured the remainder of the water into a stone bowl. He went into the cave and a couple minutes later emerged still carrying the pitcher. He poured more water into the stone bowl, not quite filling it. He placed the stone bowl carefully into a spot between two rocks so that it sat above the edge of the fire, then added the vegetables to the water. Apparently he was really going all out on this meal. Watching the meal cooking over the fire left her wondering where he got the pork from. She hadn't seen any sign of anything larger than a rodent or a bird since arriving on the island. She also knew there was a lot that she hadn't explored yet. The other side of the mountain was an area she had not explored, but that was a long walk just to explore. Yet there was still a lot on this side of the mountain to be explored, something she could only do on days when she gathered enough to eat early in the day.

He sat on a rock across the fire from her. He was taking a break, he had the look of a person who had been working and needed to take a moment to catch his breath. He didn't smile or scowl. He just sat there, holding his thoughts to himself. She could not think of anything appropriate to say when he sat. Before today the only time they spoke without harsh words was the day he invited her here for dinner. What could she possibly say? She wasn't going to bring up the past. Even if she remembered too clearly the painful things he had said. The way he painted her to be such an evil person, when all she had done was try to keep her own sanity. She couldn't be there for him the way he expected, but she didn't understand why he couldn't accept that she did what she needed to do instead of resenting her like he did.

She couldn't talk about what she was missing either. If she tried to talk about her family or her friends she would probably start crying again. Crying in front of him was something she really didn't want to do. He may have invited her to dinner, but he still did not like her, and she wasn't going to give him the satisfaction of seeing her cry again.

She looked at the fire, at the pork roasting on the spit, and the vegetables coming to a boil. She also realized she kept looking at his legs. The dark brown hair over his muscled calves, and his thighs, and she stopped herself before she looked further. Mentally she forced her eyes to return to just watching the fire and the food, swallowing against the quivering building up in her stomach. Her throat felt dry while it seemed like her mouth was watering. She tried to tell herself it was the food cooking, but she knew better. She knew she missed what it felt like to be with a man.

Once again she stopped that line of thinking. She lowered her head briefly and took a deep breath. She definitely had to do something or she might very well try to find a way to get him out of his shorts before the night was over.

"Where did you get the pork?" It was something she wondered about, and it was the safest thing she could think to talk about.

He looked up, his green gaze catching her own. He looked surprised, as if he wasn't expecting her to talk. He turned and pointed back in the general direction of her cave. "Back that way is a cliff wall. On the other side of that wall are some feral pigs."

It took a moment for her to really understand what he had said. Feral pigs could be very dangerous. She had never seen one, but it was something she had heard about. Yet he had gone over there to hunt for and bring one back. "Wasn't that dangerous?"

"Very. I had to wait about 3 hours before one of them moved off by itself. Then I had to make sure I got it with my spear so it couldn't turn and attack me." He said. "This is the first time I have tried to hunt something with a spear. I am used to hunting with a rifle."

"Why?" She asked, wondering why he risked his life.

"I needed something other than fish or crab. And I knew I could hunt." He answered with clear understanding of what she asked. "Being patient was the hard part. After that it wasn't that difficult. I waited until it was close enough so I could get a clean shot with the spear. Kept it as quick and quiet as I possibly could. Used vines to tie it up and pull it back up the wall where I gutted and quartered it so I could bring it back here.

"Before I was on this island, I probably couldn't have handled doing all that. I'm in a lot better shape, but I still wish I was back home." His voice softened as he spoke. Wistfulness filled his words.

The sound of his voice so clearly missing his home pulled on her emotions. Reminding her how much she missed her children, her friends, even her job, and just knowing she was home. She swallowed against the lump forming in her throat as the thoughts about home filled her mind. She could not speak in that moment, and if she could, she didn't know what she would say.

He stood without saying anything further and went back into the cave. He returned after only a moment carrying a clay jug larger than the one he used to get the water. He held it close to his body as if it was full.

"I debated whether or not to bring this out." he said as he indicated the jug. "I think we both need it though."

"What is it?" she asked as she watched him carefully set it down so it leaned against the rock he had sat on. It was clear that molding clay was not one of Frank's skills. She was also clearly aware that the lump was still in her throat, and it was very likely that he heard the sadness when she asked the question.

He emptied the water out of his cup and reached out indicating he wanted her cup. "I wanted something more than water to drink all the time, so I figured out how to extract juice from some of the various fruits from the grove."

The thought of fruit juice perked up her mood the moment she heard him. She couldn't imagine how much work it took for him to fill the jug. At home she would have used a juicer, but they didn't have anything like that here. She finished the last two swallows of water and handed her cup to him.

"It was an accident, but one of the fruits fermented and I found that I had a wine." Frank finished.

He poured a small amount into her cup and handed it back. She accepted it tentatively. She loved wine, and the last time she had a glass of wine was the night before she woke up on this island. She suddenly worried about drinking wine here with him. She still found her eyes on his skin. She could almost feel the tight muscles of his stomach, arms, and legs every time she looked at him. Could she really risk drinking with him?

As these thoughts passed through her mind, he poured a small amount into his cup.

He looked up at her, sadness in his green eyes. He kept his expression neutral though. "It's actually pretty good. Give it a try." He gestured with his cup, clearly recognizing that she was being tentative.

She brought the cup up to her nose so she could smell the wine first as he watched her. He held his own cup waiting for her to be the first to taste the wine. The scent was sweet. She couldn't identify which fruit he fermented to make the wine, but whichever it was it definitely had a very pleasant smell.

She took a small sip, letting the wine settle onto her tongue so she could experience it's flavor. The taste was amazing. Maybe it was because she hadn't had anything other than water to drink in more than two months. Maybe it really was that good. It didn't matter though; she was enjoying it, even if Frank made it.

"It's really good." She told him honestly.

He smiled shyly, and brought his own cup to his nose and lips the same as she did.

"I hope you don't mind me suggesting that we don't drink too much. I thought having a cup or two tonight would be good." he said. "And I think it's much better shared, than drinking it alone."

"Do you do that often?" She asked, "I mean, drink by yourself."

He coughed and chuckled at the same time. "Oh no. Just surviving here takes up enough of my time. I got pretty drunk on it the first time when I didn't realize that I was drinking wine. There were a couple other times I drank a bit more than I should have, but I don't regret it."

She took another sip of her wine, then asked, "Why?"

He picked up the jug and gestured toward her cup. She nodded, accepting more wine as he filled her cup and he answered, "because sometimes it hurts just to be here. I wanted to dull the pain."

She understood exactly what he meant. She knew how much it hurt to miss her family, her friends, and to just not be home.

She drank more of her wine and looked at the fire. The vegetables were boiling nicely. The meat appeared nearly done, and her stomach was letting her know just how hungry she really was. He looked at her when the growling of her stomach grew so loud he clearly heard it despite the natural sounds around them.

She took another sip of wine to try and hide her embarrassment while he turned his attention to checking on the meat and vegetables. She watched amazed as he used leaves to protect his hand from the hot rock, and a flat piece of wood to drain the water from the vegetables. He used the same piece of wood to hold the steaming hot vegetables as he poured them out of the stone bowl. This he left close enough to the fire to keep it from cooling as he turned his attention to the roasting pork.

As he checked the roasting pork, she could see that the dripping juices were clear, indicating that the pork was cooked through. He cut deep into the center, studied it a moment, then grabbed the ends of the stick to remove the it from the fire.

He used what appeared to be a large hunting knife to push the pork off the spit and onto the same wooden plank he had used to chop the vegetables. In moments he had sliced the pork into thin slices ready to be served.

He surprised her one more time by bringing out two clay plates and chopsticks. The workmanship of the clay plates was as poor as the mugs and pitcher, but the chopsticks looked to be really good. She had not eaten a single meal from a plate or used something other than her fingers to eat with since the day she mysteriously appeared on this island.

He filled her plate with the pork and the vegetables and handed it and a set of chopsticks to her. The sticks were smooth to the touch and clean.

"How did you get chopsticks?" She couldn't stop herself from asking.

He answered as he fixed his own plate, "I made them. I just carved enough wood away from a couple small branches, and then used sand from the beach to make them smooth."

She fit the sticks between her fingers, finding it so familiar even though it felt like such a long time since she had last used chopsticks. She knew it really hadn't been that long, but sometimes her life back home seemed a lifetime away.

Out of the corner of her eye, she saw him sit down on his same rock across from her. She couldn't wait any longer. The food smelled incredible. Her mouth was watering and her stomach threatened to growl again. She quickly snared what looked like a piece of zucchini and placed it in her mouth. The flavor burst into her mouth leaving her feeling absolute pleasure. It was the first real vegetable she had eaten in months and it was just perfect. It was slightly soft on the outside, yet slightly crisp on the inside, and had just a hint of salt in the flavoring.

She realized her eyes had closed while savoring the taste. She opened her eyes to see him watching her. "Is it good?" He asked.

She could hear the sincerity and the concern in his voice that he really had cooked a good meal. "It's amazing." She replied almost breathlessly.

She picked up a piece of the pork next. It was every bit as amazing as the vegetable. It was sweet and juicy, and cooked perfectly. She could taste the flavoring of a marinade or rub in the meat. He had outdone himself preparing this meal.

He didn't hesitate any longer. Once she had indicated she liked it, he started eating with gusto. Both of them sat quietly, just enjoying the meal one bite after the other. In moments she realized her plate was nearly empty and it seemed like he had just handed it to her. She paused to drink wine and take a breath. The meal was delicious and she was feeling incredible all through her body. It was amazing how good it felt to enjoy what she was eating.

It also felt wonderful to have a day to be able to relax. Today was the first day she could really enjoy not having to struggle to find something to eat. She wished it was as easy for her as it seemed to be for him. She felt envy that he had time to find clay and attempt to make dishes, time to extract juice to drink instead of water, and in the process make a wine. He was doing well at taking care of himself.

"Would you like some more?" His question interrupted her thoughts.

She realized her plate had only a couple pieces of meat left on it, and her cup was empty. Part of her wanted to tell him that she didn't need more, but she knew the truth. "Yes, please." She said.

The moment the words left her mouth she remembered how it was something they often said to each other. It was one of their endearments they said to each other to express how much they wanted each other. If he noticed what she had said, he didn't react.

She kept her thought's hidden from her face as he took her plate and put a second helping of pork and vegetables on it. He did the same with his own plate before he returned her plate with more food on it.

"Be sure to save room for dessert." He told her as he handed the plate to her.

The way he said dessert was so suggestive that she felt the reaction spike from her groin through her entire body. Without thinking she picked up the cup and finished her wine, the liquid flowed across a throat that felt suddenly dry.

He was right there with the wine jug as she emptied her cup. The thought that she shouldn't drink more crossed her mind as she held her cup out for him to refill. She kept her eyes on her cup as he filled it, not trusting herself to look at him at that moment. She was sure if he looked he would surely notice how flushed her face had become. She could still feel the quivering at the bottom of her stomach, moving rhythmically through her groin and into her thighs.

She put the cup down, and needed three tries to get the chopsticks to hold steady in her fingers so she could continue eating. She kept her face down toward her plate because she knew she was blushing hotly. The frustration and embarrassment helped her get her libido under some control. She managed to take a bite, and focused on chewing slower. She kept telling herself she couldn't sleep with him. There were too many hurt feelings to just have sex with him now. No matter how much she missed being with a man.

Her face felt cooler, and she knew she couldn't keep her head down the entire evening. She cautiously looked up. He was still focused on eating. She noticed he had a strange way of holding his chopsticks, like he was holding two pencils, yet he was not having any difficulty eating with them. She relaxed, hoping he hadn't noticed how red her face was. It was easier to eat knowing he wasn't watching her. At the same time, she felt disappointed that he wasn't looking at her.

She still had a small amount of food on her plate when she realized she was feeling full. It was the biggest meal she had eaten in months. Every bit of it was delicious, and she had to admit to herself that it was because of Frank. It was impressive. The work that he had done by finding and gathering fresh vegetables, by hunting a wild pig, and the hours he spent cooking the meal during the day.

As these thoughts crossed her mind, he got up and added more wood to the fire. The sun was just starting to set, leaving them in the shadow of the mountain. She shifted to sit on the ground and lean against the rock, relaxing with the pleasantly full feeling. The glow from the fire was beautiful. It was the first time she had thought of anything about this island as beautiful. The daily struggle to survive and fight loneliness left little room for her to consider the beauty of the island. The flowering plants had not escaped her notice, but they weren't a source of food.

He interrupted her thoughts with a loud inhale and sigh. It was the sound of a man who clearly had enjoyed his meal. The sound in and of itself was pleasant. It reminded her that she was with someone. For the first time in months she was spending time with a real person, and it felt really good. It was refreshing that she didn't feel so alone or lonely. He stood, walked around the fire and held out his hand for her plate.

"I can help clean up. I don't mind." She stated while handing her plate and sticks to him.

"You're my guest tonight." he replied. "Just relax."

His voice was tender, something she had not heard from him since the one time they tried to talk as friends after the relationship ended. It was nice to hear him talk in a polite tone of voice, but she realized part of her didn't trust him still. The angry man was still there under the surface. She had heard more than enough of his anger to last a lifetime.

Despite those thoughts, she was used to taking care of others, not having someone take care of her. She handed her plate to him, but she wanted to hold onto it and take care of it herself. She got up and followed as he walked a short distance away from the fire and set the plates on a flat rock. He had two clay bowls filled with water sitting on the rock and used one to rinse off both plates. She couldn't tell what he used to wipe them off, it was like some kind of cotton wadding. If it came off one of the plants around here, it would definitely be useful to find some for herself.

Without thinking, she finished drinking the wine remaining in her cup. Looking at the cup, she realized his cup was sitting near the fire, and so was the jug he poured the wine from. Quietly she went back to the fire to refresh both cups. It didn't feel like much, but she just couldn't let him do everything and serve her all night long without doing something in return. He returned as she finished filling the cups, so she stood and held his cup out for him.

"Thank you," He said with a smile of appreciation.

"Thank you, dinner was delicious." She answered.

"You're welcome then. Did you save room for dessert though?"

She felt her eyebrows rise with the surprise she felt. When he said save room for dessert the first time, she didn't really think about it. To be honest with herself, she did briefly think about him for dessert, but that is not the same thing as dinner dessert.

"Did you really fix something for dessert?"

His smile grew until his entire face lit up. "Yes I did. Wait here."

He went back to the cave and returned just a moment later carrying three bowls. He handed her two empty bowls. "Sit." He indicated the rocks by the fire.

She sat with the bowls and he sat beside her. She could feel the heat of his skin so close to her. For a moment she didn't care what was in the bowl. The thought of dropping the bowls so she could put her hands on that hot skin sounded better than what he might have in the bowl in his hands.

He used a flat stick to scoop the dessert into the first bowl she held. She switched the bowls and he scooped dessert into it as well. He handed her a flat stick like the one he scooped the dessert with.

Whatever it was smelled sweet, yet fruity. "What is it?"

"I found some sugar cane. I ground it up and sprinkled it onto some berries. I figured it would make a nice treat for our Christmas Eve dinner." He answered with the same face brightening smile.

"No Way! Are you serious? Where did you find sugar cane?" Surprise and elation pushed other thoughts out of her mind.

"When you go to the grove, they are in that field off to the left of the path. I was exploring that area and accidentally broke a stalk. It wasn't hard to realize what it was after that."

She used the stick to scoop some of the berries into her mouth. The sweetened flavor burst across her tongue. It was so intense it hit her emotions. She couldn't really remember the last time she had enjoyed a dessert. She missed moments like this. She missed chocolate, and the cakes and pies she enjoyed baking. It took just one taste of this dessert to bring it all back to her.

She couldn't imagine a time she would say Frank had done something so amazing, but he did. She still felt full from dinner, but the fruit was so delicious, she couldn't stop from eating it. After only a few bites she had to stop though. She felt so full she was sure she could burst. She looked over and noticed that he had stopped eating too. Both bowls still had several bites of dessert left.

"I guess I should have waited a little longer before bringing out dessert." he said as he shifted on his seat.

"It was delicious. Thank you." Politeness stronger than all other feelings she felt toward him.

The smile still kept his face lit up. She couldn't help herself but to smile with him. She realized she was sitting close to him where the heat from his skin seemed even more intense. That intensity seeped deep into her, and she wanted it. The throbbing deep below her stomach was pulsing out through every fiber of her being, and she wanted it. She felt so alive with every pulse.

She started with how sudden and intense that feeling came on. She couldn't remember the last time she had gone so long without being with a man unless she intentionally chose it for herself. A good looking man was sitting beside her close enough to feel the heat from his body. The long hair, beard and mustache gave him a rugged look she wasn't used to. It just added to him though, like it was naturally part of him. The leaner muscles fit his frame very nicely too. He was clearly stronger here than he was when they dated.

She remembered the man he was. He was normal in so many ways. He was smart, ambitious, and not afraid to take on a challenge. Physically he was soft though. Too many days of sitting in an air conditioned office had taken a toll on his muscles. Those muscles had definitely come out nicely on this island, and they looked deliciously strong. Her hands itched to reach out, caress his skin and feel those firm muscles.

She held back though. Part of her still remembered that painful breakup between them. After divorcing her second husband, she tried getting back with the now ex-husband and having sex with him. The sex was good still, but it didn't help her heart heal from the divorce. She acknowledged Frank was there for her and played a part helping her heart heal. He was going through his own huge emotional pain, and he let her be there for him. It was like that was what she really needed back then. To just be there for someone. He needed more than she could give though, and she had her own needs that he just wasn't going to be able to meet then.

Maybe it was different now. She hadn't seen or spoken to him in years before finding him here on this island. He was so angry seeing her here, but maybe he had changed. He certainly did a wonderful job with dinner, and with letting her just relax and enjoy the evening. Even before the island, she couldn't remember the last time a man treated her to dinner like this. It was actually very romantic.

She looked up to the sky to see that it still had some blue from twilight, but was quickly turning to star filled black. The moon was full and growing brighter as it rose into the night sky.

Lust won out. The continuous throbbing between her legs had finally beat down her internal resistance. Frank stood up just as she was about to reach out to touch him. She couldn't move as he turned and reached toward her. With disappointment, she watched as he picked up her bowl, turned and walked to where he washed the plates earlier. Didn't he realize he could have her? Didn't he realize that if he would kiss her, she would just melt?

Despite the trembling in her legs, she stood, walked over to him and kneeled beside him. The bowls were much harder to see than the plates were earlier, but he patiently rinsed them. She picked up the pitcher of water and poured more for him. He shook the bowls and sticks free of water, then stacked everything together and picked it all up. "Do you prefer to open Christmas presents on Christmas Eve, or Christmas day?"

"We usually wait until Christmas morning." She answered. As the words came out, she realized what he really meant. With a shock she realized she didn't have a gift for him, but he had a gift for her. It was like a splash of cold water on her libido to realize he meant to give her a gift when she didn't have something to give him in return. How in the world could she possibly come up with something to give him on this Island?

She followed him back to the campfire.

"I don't have wrapping paper, and honestly it isn't much." he said while setting the dishes on the rock where they were sitting earlier. "We wait for Christmas day too; except we open one gift on Christmas Eve."

She sensed something change in him when he said that. He stopped talking after mentioning Christmas Eve. He looked like he was remembering other Christmas days. She stayed quiet and let him have his thoughts.

"I'm sorry. You know it gets difficult sometimes. Anyway, I wanted to say that we may be pretty busy tomorrow. I thought about waiting, and I thought about giving you your gift tonight." He sorted out the dishes on the rock as he spoke.

She didn't look at him directly, giving him a kind of privacy as he continued. She liked hearing his voice. The endless days of not hearing any voice other than her own seemed to suck the life out of her sometimes.

"Will you accept your gift tonight? So we can focus on what we need to do tomorrow." he asked her.

She understood what he meant. Every day here they both needed to find something to eat and take care of their shelters. He definitely made today better. The only problem was that she didn't have a gift for him. She would definitely have to come up with an idea, and quick. "Sure."

He picked up the dishes she had used, and held them out. He even included the chopsticks and the flat stick she used with dessert. Her hands trembled slightly as she accepted the gifts. She didn't have anything like them. It didn't matter if they were crudely made, they were beautiful. She didn't have to burn her fingers trying to eat. She had something to eat from, instead of using a stick or a flat rock.

"Merry Christmas." he whispered.

She looked up and caught his eyes. "Merry Christmas." She whispered back.

He broke the eye contact first. She returned to looking at the treasure she held in her hands. Out of the corner of her eye she saw him bend down to pick something up. "Don't forget your cup." She realized he was holding her cup out for her, and she saw it was filled again.

Smiling she carefully set her gifts down on the rock and accepted the cup. Wordlessly they tapped the cups and drank.

"Thank you Frank. This is the first time I've been able to relax since I found myself on this Island."

"You're welcome." His answer was soft, but sincere.

They continued to sip their wine; the fire was dying down, leaving the area bathed in moonlight instead of firelight.

The last sip of wine slipped from the cup and onto her tongue. She considered getting more, but her body wanted something else instead. She wanted him to make his next move and finish seducing her. To be plain, she wanted him to just grab her, pull her in close and kiss her until her toes curled. Was she going to have to make the next move to let him know he had won tonight?

Won? Why would she think that way? Was this a contest where he won by seducing her? It didn't really matter. Either he was going to have his way with her body, or she was going to just take him and make sure he had the greatest night she could give him to thank him for tonight.

The last thought made her pause. He did deserve it. Ever since dessert she had been waiting for him to finish seducing her, but he deserved it. He deserved to be thoroughly kissed, to have his body thoroughly ravished until the sun came up with him smiling brighter than ever. Just the thought of running her hands and lips over all his skin sent throbbing thrills through her entire body.

With two steps she was close to him. She could feel his heat radiating against her own skin. Her hand reached out to his forearm. The course hair rubbed against her fingers. The muscles felt as firm as she imagined they would feel. Just the feel of him caused her breathing to pause, followed by a slight gasp of air.

"Michelle?" he broke the silence.

She looked up into his eyes. They were glittering from the moonlight. She knew they were green, but it was too dark to see them now. She imagined her own brown eyes must appear as pure black to him.

"Please don't." he continued.

She felt her heart miss a beat. Her hand remained on his forearm, unwilling to move away from having that contact. "I don't understand. Don't you want me? Isn't this why you brought me up here and fixed dinner for me?" She asked

"No." he stated.

She pulled her hand back as if he had scorched her. Her entire body tensed, ready to run away in embarrassment. How could she have been so wrong about his intentions? How did she misread the signals so badly?

"I mean to say I wanted you here to share dinner. I didn't want to be alone on Christmas Eve, and I thought you wouldn't want to be alone either. I didn't do this to seduce you. That part of our lives is behind us." He continued.

"Are you serious?" She couldn't hide her irritation. "You've been here longer than me and you don't want the only woman available to you? Even when she is ready to throw herself at you?" She realized she was breathing fast when she finished.

He stepped back away from her, putting space and the fire pit between them. She noticed he wouldn't even look at her now. What was wrong with her? Why was he doing this? Did he just have some sick and twisted desire to keep punishing her for what he thought she did wrong?

"My feelings toward you haven't changed. I meant what I said about a truce. I will keep that truce no matter what."

She took a breath to interrupt.

"Please don't interrupt." he said sternly. "I didn't bring you up here to argue with you. I can tell you are irritated by your voice. Please don't argue tonight. Or please just let me know you need to return to your own cave."

She felt her body trembling all over. She wanted him still, and she was angry with him, and angry at herself for wanting him. For the first time in months she felt like this wasn't the most miserable place on the earth to be, and in a flash it was the most miserable place on the earth to be.

She couldn't stay now. She couldn't stay around a man who just made it clear he didn't want her around. She couldn't stay around someone who hated her, not even if he could set that hatred aside for Christmas. He still hated her.

"I think it would be best that I go back to my cave." Her voice was tightly controlled. She turned to leave and walked three steps before his voice stopped her again.

"Don't forget your things. They are yours now." he reminded her.

Part of her wanted to leave them, but she knew how much it would mean to have them. She felt a tear fall down her cheek as she turned to pick them up. "Thank you. Thank you for dinner and thank you for the presents."

She kept her head down as she spoke. He didn't need to see her crying again.

She felt him watching as she walked away, carefully going back down the hillside to her own cave. Mentally she was glad for the full moon. She probably couldn't have walked down this path if it had been full dark. Once back in her own cave, she set the presents aside and laid down on her blanket. All of the emotions and frustration poured out in her tears until she fell asleep.

> You know how the time flies.
> Only yesterday was the time of our lives.
> We were born and raised in a summer haze
> Bound by the surprise of our glory days
> - Someone Like You by Adele

The next morning Michelle found several pieces of raw pork sitting beside her fire pit. It was more than she could possibly eat before it could spoil. She knew it was from the pig that Frank had killed earlier, and the message was that it was more than he could eat also. Today was Christmas day and he promised her a truce through today. As much as it hurt to be rejected last night, her conscience wouldn't let her go the day without doing something to repay his kindness for dinner and the gifts.

Quickly she put the pork on one of the clay plates and carefully set it in the water so that the pork wasn't actually in the water. Hopefully the water would keep the plate and pork cool so that it would last longer and give her time to fix dinner for Frank. There were several fruits in the grove that she could mix with the pork to create a dish that should be just right for Christmas dinner. Some of the plants growing in the area that she knew were safe to eat could probably be added as well for seasoning.

If he was willing to share some vegetables, she could probably put a nice stew together. Just imagining a stew made her mouth water in a pleasant way. The thought was enough to spur her into action. She needed to find him and talk to him about cooking dinner.

He was sitting outside his cave leaning against the rocks when she arrived. He didn't get up or move, but he did look and notice that she arrived. He looked so sad the way he was sitting there. The look on his face caused her to pause and swallow. Mentally she prayed he would keep the truce and let her cook dinner for both of them. "Frank. Do we still have a truce through today?"

"Yes." The sound of his voice was thick with sorrow indicative that something really was wrong. She felt a need in her heart to reach out to him and comfort him, but at the same time she wanted to turn and walk away and just leave him to his pain. She knew she did not want to get emotionally involved with him again, but she couldn't deny that she reached out to people in need.

"I'm sorry if I'm intruding. I wanted to ask if I could cook today's dinner?"

He shifted and turned so he was facing her while still sitting. "I think that would be nice." His voice had fallen to almost a whisper. Whatever was on his mind was something he was struggling to hold in and his body language said he was losing that battle.

"Would it be ok for me to bring my things and cook here? Also, do you have any more of those vegetables?" Inside she felt her heart sinking. She hated standing here asking him questions when he either needed to be alone or needed someone to hold him.

He sighed audibly, "Yeah, I don't mind, and there are more vegetables."

She tried to push her tension away. "Ok. I'll go and get what I need. I should get started around midday. Will that be ok?"

"Yeah. I'll set the vegetables out for you."

She nodded at his response, but couldn't tell if he noticed or not. His mood was so strong that she felt a lump in her throat in response to his emotions. Quietly she turned and went back down the trail, her emotions torn and twisted inside. She felt so helpless. He was clearly hurting deeply and she couldn't do anything to help him. At the same time she hated that part of her really didn't care how much he was hurting. After all the times he had hurt her, she just couldn't make herself care for him again, and yet she did care for him. Maybe after dinner they could try talking. For whatever reason that had never worked before, but it was the only thing she could think to try.

As she walked along the path, her thoughts went over the possibilities of what was bothering him. The worst thought that crossed her mind was that he was really angry and upset with her for ruining their evening the night before. If that was the case, then she was going to give her best to make it up to him today. Just cook a meal for him so that he could relax and nothing more. No attempting to seduce him, and no asking him for anything he wasn't willing to give.

If he was sad because today was Christmas and he was stuck here on this island, then she could certainly relate to how he felt. The tears she had cried the past few days were definite testament to how much it hurt missing her family today.

The part of her that didn't care about him kept bugging her, but she pushed it down. He was nothing but nice to her last night and she repaid him by ruining the evening. If they go back to hating and not speaking to each other tomorrow, then so be it, but today she decided she was going to pay back his kindness for yesterday, and if possible make up for her behavior last night.

With resolution and determination she went to the grove hoping to find a pineapple ripe and ready to be cooked with the pork waiting at her cave. Frank promised to set out vegetables, and unfortunately she didn't know what he had. She knew some of the fruits on the island were different than what she expected. She hoped whatever he provided would be something she was used to. If he provided the same vegetables that he cooked last night, it might work to make a stew. The stone bowl he used for cooking would be perfect for simmering a nice stew. The very thought set her mouth watering and her stomach grumbled with anticipation.

In the grove she found three pineapples that seemed ripe. She wasn't used to growing and picking her own food. The growing season where she lived was never more than three months long, and was more likely to be just under two months. If she could afford a decent greenhouse, she could extend the growing season to about 6 months, but that was the most she was going to get before it was too cold for even a greenhouse to be of much use. They did look like what she was used to finding in the produce section of the supermarket though. Using as much care as she could manage to avoid poking her hands with the spiky leaves, she tilted the pineapple to the side and reached in to cut it free.

Turning around she noticed the cherry tree she had found the second day she was on the island. It wasn't the only cherry tree in the grove, but it's cherries were the sweetest. Inspired by the thought she went to the cherry tree which had cherries that were slightly tart. Once cooked with the pineapple and pork, the tartness would enhance the flavor of the pork. With cherries safely tucked in the front of her shirt, she carried the pineapple back to her cave.

The pork was cool to the touch where she left it in the water. Later in the day, sunlight would hit this part of the spring. She intended to be back at Frank's cave before then, so she would not need to worry about the temperature of the pork right now. There was one plant she found with leaves that she could use for seasoning. The flavor reminded her of cilantro, but like so many other things she had tasted here, the taste wasn't quite the same. Hopefully it would provide a nice addition to the pork.

Despite an initial balancing issue, she did manage to gather up all the materials and carry them up the hill to Frank's cave. He wasn't in sight when she arrived, so she set everything down on the wood plank table he was using last night to chop vegetables. She looked at the vegetables sitting on the table waiting for her. Frank kept his promise to provide vegetables. She stared amazed at what she was sure were potatoes, carrots, and celery stalks. He had also put out four small clay bowls. One had some salt, two had what appeared to be crushed leaves, and the last contained what looked like dried rosemary. The crushed leaves clearly smelled like fresh herbs, but she couldn't identify them just by look and smell.

How long had he been here? Judging by his appearance he was probably here months before she woke up here, but all these things suggested he had been here longer than she guessed. He was making this his home. Did he know what to look for when he found these? Or were these things the product of searching over time? He already admitted the salt was not easy to make, and he provided a small bowl of it for her to use.

The ingredients held her attention as she thought about how to make use of them. The possibilities were numerous. Years spent cooking in the upscale restaurant gave her numerous ideas for how to use the ingredients. Unfortunately she didn't have the ovens, cookware, and other things needed for all those ideas. While thinking she began pacing, letting her mind wander as her feet walked around the fire pit. The stone bowl sat upside down beside the fire pit and sticks used for skewering lay next to the bowl.

He roasted the pork the night before and she really wanted to do something different with it today. She looked at the stone bowl, and turned it over. It was hard to tell, but she guessed it would hold four quarts or more. That would mean it was more than large enough to simmer a stew. Her mouth watered again as she remembered the idea she first had this morning. It was perfect and she smiled at the thought.

Hot coals remained in the fire pit, and broken wood sat a few feet away ready to be burned. She placed tinder and wood in the fire pit and in moments smoke was rising from the wood sitting on the hot coals. She blew into the smoke, making the coals glow until they heated the wood and caught fire. It felt satisfying to start a fire without having to use her flint and steel.

He returned just as the fire was getting going. He was carrying what appeared to be a pouch filled with something. As she looked at it, she realized it was probably made from a t-shirt. That would explain why he walked around shirtless. Using the shirt as a pouch was clearly practical, and it made her seriously consider using one of her shirts the same way. That would be a tough choice, she had only three shirts, and all three were showing wear from being worn so much in the jungle. At this rate she wouldn't have any shirts in less than a year. But the pouch looked like a really good idea, one she couldn't set aside without giving it more thought.

He paused and watched her working on the fire and noted the preparations she was making for the meal. His face was a mask hiding the emotions he felt earlier in the morning. She sensed those emotions were still present, and her best guess was that he looked thoughtful while he watched.

With a start, she realized she was staring, and pulled her eyes away from his face. The fire would need wood shortly to really get it going, but for now she needed to focus on the meal or dinner would be very late. She grabbed the stone bowl and found it was heavier than she realized, but it felt very sturdy in her hands. "Where can I get some water?" She asked.

He was sitting and sorting out nuts and berries from the pouch. Where did he find those treasures? Quickly he wiped his hands on the legs of his shorts, got up and went into his cave only to return a moment later with one of the pitchers she saw last night. "I guess I didn't think of everything you would need." He commented sheepishly.

"It's ok. I can't believe everything you have here already. This is amazing." She felt a blush creeping into her cheeks as she talked about the things he had set out. With her mind racing, she pushed those feelings back down. She wasn't here to seduce him, that was a bad enough mistake last night. It was Christmas day, and he really deserved a good meal in return for the meal she had yesterday.

The pitcher held more than enough water for her to fill the stone bowl half way. Quickly she worked on the carrots and celery and added them to the water. The pork came next, followed by salt and two of the seasonings. He had added wood to the fire as she worked on the vegetables. The blaze was going nicely and it was beginning to form the coals she needed to truly simmer the stew. She placed the stone bowl between the two rocks that kept it suspended over the fire. She would have to watch it carefully and monitor the heat so it wouldn't scald.

With the stew over the fire she turned her attention to the pineapple and realized exactly what she wanted to do with it. She hadn't had a chance to work with a fresh pineapple in a long time, but the skills were still there. In moments the skin was cut away and she had chunks of fresh pineapple sitting in front of her. She placed one of the small chunks into her mouth and the sweet flavor of perfectly ripe pineapple burst onto her tongue. A smile formed at the delight of successfully getting a ripe pineapple. The knife wasn't the best for chopping, but it was more than adequate for the job of dicing the pineapple in to small relish size bits. The cherries followed and were just as easily chopped into small bits as well.

She tested the herbs he had supplied by smell and taste. One of them has a slightly tangy flavor which felt right. She chopped up the green leaves into tiny pieces and added them to the cherry and pineapple mix. The clay bowl provided was nearly overflowing with the mixture, which made stirring it difficult. Some of the mix fell out onto the cutting surface as she stirred, but there was more than enough.

While she worked on the stew and pineapple relish, Frank had clearly been busy working as well. She heard the distinct sounds of chopping wood as he worked to keep his wood supply stocked. A brief stab of jealousy filled her stomach as she thought about how much work she put into finding branches and twigs small enough for her to be able to break them for her own small fire. Once again she pushed those thoughts down. He didn't owe her anything, and as much as she hated having to work on her own, she had to accept that he was free to choose his own path, despite how much it hurt for him to do so.

She closed her eyes on that last thought. She hadn't thought of it in that manner before, but it was true. His actions and the deliberate way he had avoided her, really had hurt. It probably hurt more that he wanted nothing to do with her than his refusal to help. That was crazy, but it was true. Every day was an intense struggle to stay alive and she didn't have any help, but it hurt more that the only man anywhere around her didn't want to have anything to do with her except for today.

Those thoughts had to be put aside, she quietly said in her mind. She grabbed the first potato and began washing the dirt off it. She focused on what she was doing to keep her mind distracted from thinking about what was or was not happening between her and Frank. The feel of the potato skins was familiar to her hands, and it was unexpectedly comforting to sit and wash them clean. Once they were clean, she put them on the wooden plank used for a chopping surface.

She saw the spot where Frank stacked wood for the fire. He was a few yards away chopping more wood. As he chopped the wood, he threw it haphazardly onto a pile. It was clear he was going to bring it closer to the fire and stack it neatly with the rest of the wood he had gathered. Quietly she got up and went to gather the wood and bring it back to stack it for him. It wasn't much, especially compared to what he had given her yesterday, but it was something she could do for him.

Picking up the first pieces of wood she looked at him chopping the next piece free. His skin was covered in a sheen of sweat. Even his hair was damp from sweating so freely. Despite that he continued working. The muscles in his arms and back were rippling, moving freely with each swing. Somehow he had made a stone axe and fashioned a handle for it, the handle didn't have the smooth look of extended use, leading her to think he had replaced it recently.

As she walked back toward the fire pit with an arm load of wood, she wanted very much to turn back around and watch him working. He looked really good covered with sweat and the way his muscles were moving under his skin had her heart beating faster. She gulped against a throat that felt suddenly dry. The wood had its place and with barely a thought she stacked it. The day was going to be very long and would thoroughly test her resolve not to try and seduce him if she kept watching him working.

Despite her resolve to try and be good, she did look at him. Every time she went to gather an armload of wood she looked at his lean legs holding his body steady with each swing. She looked at his biceps flex as he pulled the ax up for the next swing. She watched a drop of sweat roll down the sun darkened skin of his back and make its way down to the waist band of his shorts.

There wasn't any more wood on the ground to be picked up and moved to the stack. She looked at the ground feeling like she was in a daze. She barely remembered the trips back and forth to move the freshly chopped wood.

He stopped chopping, his shoulders rising and falling with his heavy breathing. The wood pile was measurably higher than when they started. Envy passed through her body looking at the piled wood. Back at her own cave, she had a small pile of sticks inside the cave, and a slightly larger, but still small pile of sticks by her fire pit. The meager sticks were all she was capable of gathering, and she couldn't build her fires big, lest she use up all of her wood and have to start over from scratch. Sometimes it meant cooking took longer than she wanted.

Looking back, she saw him sitting with his eyes closed, still breathing heavily, but already she could see that he was getting his breath back. He didn't really look tired, just momentarily winded. Quietly she went back to the fire pit to check on the progress of the stew. It was simmering nicely and already she could smell how well it was coming along. The pineapple relish was macerating nicely, it already was forming a gel around the bits and pieces.

From the corner of her eye she saw him get up and come back to the cave, he passed by without a word, entering his cave and disappearing into the shadows. Moments later he returned carrying a towel. "I'll be back in a few minutes. Do you need anything?"

She shook her head as she answered, "No, everything is cooking and should be ready in a couple hours."

He nodded then turned and walked the opposite direction of the trail back down to her cave. She watched as he walked around the curving rock wall that formed this side of the mountain. It was clear he was going to wash up before dinner, which was understandable. His hair hung limply down to his shoulders and sweat streaked his skin. For a moment she considered following him to see where he was going to wash up, but dinner was over the fire and she didn't want to risk ruining it.

Sitting and watching the simmering stew, she thought about the potatoes. Normally she would wrap them in aluminum foil and put them in the coals to cook, but that option wasn't available. In some places, they used leaves to wrap things in for cooking. She wasn't sure what kind of leaves she could use that would protect the potatoes as they cooked. A baking oven would be really helpful.

The thought of a baking oven made her think about how people used to bake things, in the days before they had modern ovens, or even coal burning ovens. They made their own stone ovens heated by their fires. Could she do something like that here?

There were lots of rocks in various shapes and sizes around his fire pit, and on the ground outside his cave. She stood and walked around looking at the rocks. Scattered around she found what she hoped she could find, four flat rocks and two rocks with a squared off side that were about the same size.

Back on the trail down the hill, she remembered a bush with large heavy leaves. She went back to that bush and cut off one leaf for each potato. She placed the largest flat rock in the fire pit, setting it directly on top of some coals, then put the two squared rocks spaced apart on top of the flat rock. She salted two potatoes, wrapped them in the leaves, and placed them between the squared rocks. The three flat rocks formed a roof and sides to create an oven to bake the potatoes. Feeling proud of what she had just done, she added wood to fire to heat up her little oven. The potatoes would probably be finished baking by the time the stew was done. Dinner was definitely coming along very nicely.

He returned just as the fire over the oven was building up. She looked up at him and smiled. She couldn't help but smile in that moment, she felt good inside and knew she had just done something that he hadn't. He looked cleaner and refreshed, his hair was wet, but hanging cleanly. He responded to her smile with a small smile of his own. Still smiling, he took his towel to hang it over a nearby branch to dry.

As she stirred the stew, enjoying the smell of it simmering, he took the water pitcher into his cave and returned with it filled. He filled the two clay mugs with fresh water and handed one to her. The water was cool and refreshing. She didn't realize how thirsty she was until the water hit her throat. Both of them drained their mugs, refilled them and drained them again.

They sat, quietly for the moment. Relaxing and not worrying about what needed to be done. They had dinner for today. He brought out the nuts and berries and shared them with her. The few bites quieted the rumbling in her stomach, but the real meal was still to come.

She thought about the things she wanted to say and things she wanted to ask. Where did he find the vegetables? Would he share? Could they try to work together? Surely there was something she could do to help him and make surviving easier. Why was he so sad this morning? He didn't seem upset about last night, but he could be hiding his feelings. That would be easy enough to do since he was staying so quiet.

Despite all the thoughts going through her mind, she couldn't think of anything to say, and so she sat quietly, occasionally checking on the stew, or adding wood to keep the fire around her make shift oven hot. Whatever he was thinking, he was keeping it to himself, and remaining just as quiet. She alternated between feeling uncomfortable with the silence and accepting it.

A loud grumbling in her stomach pulled her from her thoughts. She looked to see if he heard her stomach growling. He wasn't looking at her, but she clearly heard his stomach growling as she looked at him. He did turn to look then, both realizing how hungry they were. She couldn't help but laugh lightly, and he laughed with her.

Smiling she checked on the stew. The carrots and celery were tender. Using one of the cut sticks, she moved the fire and coals away from the bowl. Carefully she used the stick to move one of the rocks from her oven, and used the cooking stick to prod the potatoes. The leaves covering them were dry and brown, and the potatoes inside were nice and tender to her prodding stick.

"I think dinner is ready." She announced with a smile.

He responded by getting two clay plates and the leaves he used to protect his hands. Carefully he pulled out the two potatoes and set one on each plate. She pulled her knife out and began skinning the searing hot potatoes. The steam burned her fingers as she worked, but she didn't complain. Once peeled, she used the flat stick used for stirring to mash the potatoes and form them into a mashed potato bowl on each plate.

With his help, they poured the stew into the potato bowls. She added the pineapple relish to each plate. They each took their plates and sat to enjoy the meal she had cooked. The flat sticks were not as good as a spoon and fork, but they were good enough to allow them to scoop up the potatoes and stew.

The stew and potato mix hit her tongue with an amazing burst of flavor. It was just perfect, exactly what she was in the mood for. The relish added a spicy sweetness to each bite that made it even better. He started eating tentatively, uncertain of what she had made, but after a couple bites he didn't hold back from enjoying the meal thoroughly.

She caught him looking at her make shift oven. She could sense he was admiring what she had done, and possibly thinking about how useful it would be. She looked at it as well, thinking that she was going to figure out how to make another for her own fire pit.

"This is delicious," his words interrupted her thoughts. "Using the rocks to bake the potatoes was an amazing idea. I wish I had thought of something like that."

"Thank you," she couldn't think of anything else to say and didn't try to fill in any more conversation.

As if in agreement, he also didn't speak further, but continued to eat until his plate was clean. In moments she realized her plate was also clean. She felt satisfyingly full, not overstuffed like yesterday. Together they cleaned the plates and bowls she used. They ate almost all of the stew, so he carried the bowl away from camp to empty it and brought it back to be cleaned.

The sun was still up, she figured they had a couple more hours of daylight before sunset. He brought the wine out and filled each of their cups. She accepted the wine, promising she wouldn't drink as much as she did the night before.

"I want to show you something," he said and motioned his hand for her to follow.

"Ok," she said in response and followed. He led her the way he went earlier to wash up. A few yards along the trail and she saw that the rocks along the rock wall became broken. He reached a spot where he could climb up those rocks and proceeded to climb. She followed, but did admit to herself that she stopped once or twice too to look up at him and admire the view of his body. The climb was easy, as if the rocks were broken in such a way to become steps instead of merely broken rocks. They reached a flat shelf where they could easily sit.

She sat down beside him and the view took her breath away. They had climbed high enough to where they could see over the trees surrounding Frank's cave. She had an amazing view of the cove she saw the first day she arrived on the island. The same waterfall she saw that day poured in white cascades to the ocean below. The waves crashed against the sheer cliff inside the cove. Lush green grass and jungle lined the top of the cliff, leaving her unable to see where the water came from. "It's beautiful." She whispered with admiration in her voice.

He didn't respond. She turned to him and saw that he was looking out over the ocean. She followed his eyes and saw what he was looking at. There was another island so far away it was just a shadow above the water. The distance was too far to gage, but she knew instinctively there was no way to reach that island without a boat.

"Do you think there could be people there?" She asked him.

"I don't know." He answered. "Have you noticed there are no trails in the sky?"

She looked up in response to his question. She saw a few white fluffy clouds, and pure blue sky. "What do you mean trails?"

He looked up too. "Airplanes." He paused while the one word sank in. "Everywhere I have ever been I could look up and see white trails left behind by airplanes crossing the world. There aren't any here. I've looked numerous times, and I've not once seen the trails left by an airplane. I've stared at the ocean for hours from this spot, and from the beach below. I've never seen any sign of boats. No trash, no trails in the water. It makes me feel like I am the last man on earth."

The words sank into her heart. The sky held no signs of anything made by man. There was nothing there except for the clouds and the sky. The water was the same story. Could it really be that somehow they were the last people on earth? She swallowed against the lump in her throat. "Do you really think we are the last?" She couldn't stop herself from answering the question.

"No. I can't believe that. I'm sure we are someplace far from anyone else though." He answered.

The idea of being so far away that they couldn't see any sign of other people wasn't much better than the thought of being the last people on earth. Somehow she needed to change the subject. "Why were you so sad this morning?"

He sat quietly. She turned and looked at him. She saw it in his face, the sadness was still there. He had kept it hidden while they worked and had dinner. She felt sorry she asked the question. She shouldn't have reminded him of whatever it was that was so heavy on his heart.

"Your daughter. She's about twenty two or twenty three years old now isn't she?" he asked.

"You have a good memory, she's twenty two." His question brought Zoey's face immediately to her mind. Her daughter was her youngest child. Both of her children were probably worried sick wondering where their mother was. She imagined them searching for her day and night, and even fantasized about them finding her here and rescuing her.

"My son's mother passed away when he was just eight years old. He's twelve now, and today is the first time he is spending Christmas without either of his parents." His voice was choked with emotion as he said the words.

The words hit her heart with a wave of emotions. Frank's son was just a child. He couldn't look for his own father, and he had already lost his mother. Wherever he was, he was living with someone other than either of his own parents, and being cared for by people who might be strangers. She knew how much she missed her children, but they were adults and they were taking care of themselves. Both lived on their own, without assistance from either parent. If they really needed to, they could call on their father. Frank's son didn't have any of that, and she had completely forgotten about his son. She couldn't stop the lump from forming in her throat, or the tear from falling down her cheek as she felt the intense sadness that must be in Frank's heart knowing that he couldn't be there for his son.

She got up on her knees and pulled his head onto her shoulder. "I'm sorry," she whispered into his hair.

Once again he didn't say anything, as if there were no words that could be said at that moment. He didn't pull away, letting her hold him and provide what comfort she could. Feeling the heat of his body, and his head in her arms made the loneliness of the situation even more intense. Was this really the last day of Frank's truce? Was he going to return to pushing her away again? Wasn't there anything she could say that would convince him to work together?

She felt the dampness of his tears on her breast. She stopped thinking and just held him as he cried. Her own tears fell into his hair as her emotions matched his. She hated this island, she hated being away from her children. She hated not being home. She hated that he was hurting so much more than she was right now. She hated every day they had fought, and hated not knowing what tomorrow would be like. The emotions burned through her chest, and ruled her mind as the tears flowed freely from both of them. The sound of the waves came back to her ears as the tears began to slow. She sniffled against her running nose to keep it from making a mess in Frank's hair, and pulled back when she realized her efforts were going to be futile. Shifting made her realize that her knees were hurting because of the rock underneath them. Reluctantly she moved to sit down beside him and let her knees have a much needed break. Neither spoke for several minutes as they allowed their tears to dry and the emotions to calm down. She broke the silence first.

"Is the truce really going to end tomorrow?" She had to know what was going to happen next.

"Yes." He stated flatly, despite the emotions still evident in his voice.

"Why? We did a good job of working together yesterday and today."

He paused before answering. "Answering your question risks an argument tonight. Do you really want to know?"

She kept her eyes on the cove below, forcing her emotions into a calm state. She needed to know and she needed to accept not arguing with him. They both were hurting and she couldn't be responsible for either of them hurting more.

She nodded without looking at him, "yes, I want to know." Maybe if she knew she could try to fix whatever was wrong.

"Very well. To put it simply, I don't like you. I don't like how you treated me, and I don't trust you." His voice was calm as he said those words. They were not a revelation. His actions for the past couple months, and even before then had made it clear. Hearing them made it more real though.

"I see. You don't think this is something we can get past? Or maybe just put it aside while we are here?"

Once again he was quiet. She could feel him beside her, but she didn't know if he was looking at her, or somewhere else. She couldn't tell if he was thinking, or just not answering the question. She focused on the sound of the crashing waves as she waited for his answer.

"I don't want to. If we try, it's just a matter of time before we are fighting again, and I can't do that anymore." He finally said in response.

The emotions in his voice came through clearly. Whatever it was, he was still upset and hurting. Yesterday and today were a very welcome relief from the daily efforts for survival, but they were a brief break. Tomorrow she would have to go back to working on her own to take care of herself until somehow they could be rescued. There were no tears inside of her heart, she somehow knew this is how it would turn out. She got to enjoy two days of him being nice to her. Their lives were separate until they ended up on this island, and their lives would continue to be separate even here.

The conversation turned to topics easier to talk about. Neither wanted to discuss the families they missed, and neither wanted to discuss the end of the truce. As the sun reached the horizon they left the rocky shelf and returned to his cave. He used vines to gather up two large bundles of wood and helped her carry them back to her cave. She tried to refuse, but he pointed out that she helped and had earned it.

He left her at her cave as darkness was quickly settling on the island. There was still enough light to see the trail. Neither said good bye, they simply acknowledged that the truce was over and tomorrow they would go back to not speaking to each other or helping each other.

> I lose my way
> And it's not too long before you point it out
> I cannot cry
> Because I know that's weakness in your eyes
> - Because of You by Reba McEntire

The days passed into weeks which passed into months. Stretches of time passed without any sign of Frank on the island, and other days they passed each other in their daily struggle for survival. The skills needed to survive became honed with use. She didn't figure out his knack for creating tools such as the stone axe, but she did manage to make use of what she could find. She found a sharp flat rock that she could to some degree use for breaking smaller branches. She built up her fire pit so that it had an oven sitting over one side.

In all the days she watched, and noticed what he had pointed out on Christmas day. There was no sign of any other people to be seen. She didn't once see any evidence of an airplane in the sky. No matter how high she climbed the mountain she didn't see any sign of boats on the ocean. She was able to climb high enough to see much of the island they were on. The section they lived in was only a small part of the island, and it was blocked off from the rest of the island by the mountain they lived on and by a rock wall that extended from the island to the ocean on the other side. She didn't venture to explore the other side of the rock wall. The idea of confronting a wild beast was enough to keep her on this side of the wall.

Useful items could be found within the jungle. She found a plant with thorns at the tips of its broad leaves. One of the thorns caught on her shirt, tearing the shirt, but at the same time the thorn broke away followed by strings from the plant. Frustrated about the tear in her shirt she almost threw it away, but realized it was like an instant needle and thread which worked wonderfully to repair the torn shirt, and a couple other tears in her clothes. The vines Frank used to tie the bundles of wood proved very resilient and easy to find a few yards into the jungle. Broad leaves could be formed into pouches or used to cover her plates. They proved to be water resistant enough that she could cover her fire pit and protect it on the rainy days.

The storms were too harsh and she couldn't find anything to protect her fire when those blew in. When trees blocked the path, he came down and chopped them apart and cleared the path. He didn't say anything, and she didn't either, but she often found wood that was cut short enough for her to use in her fire pit. It was obvious he was helping, just as it was obvious he was avoiding contact with her. The only time she really saw him was when they were both fishing. He didn't look at her or talk even then. She missed having someone to talk to. Those two days of conversation with him helped, but they didn't truly diminish the loneliness she felt every day. At times she considered creating something to talk to like Tom Hanks did with the volleyball in the movie Castaway. When she imagined Frank catching her talking to an inanimate object, she pushed the thought away.

It didn't stop her from trying to have a conversation with a seagull one day when she was out catching a crab. Out of courtesy for the gull being such a good listener she threw part of the crab she caught in its direction. The bird squawked what sounded like either surprise or thanks, and hesitantly took the prize she offered. In moments it sped away with the portion of crab as if afraid she would take it away. With dinner in hand she returned to her cave without anyone or anything to talk to.

The next morning she went out exploring. Since discovering that there were vegetables growing on the island she resolved to find them. At first she wanted to ask where to find them, but the truce ended and with it the opportunity to ask him. The sugar cane was easy to find since he had told her where it was. The wall that separated this part of the island from the rest was even easier to find. From there she spotted the wild pigs he had hunted for their Christmas dinner. Looking at them shuffling around for their own food set her mouth to watering. It was a nice thought, but she knew she didn't stand a chance of killing one of them without putting herself at serious risk. Thus she found herself back in the jungle searching.

With the grove at her back, she pushed through broad leaves which brushed her legs in the shadowy recess of this part of the jungle. The area was so dense she could see only small patches of the ground below. Ahead she looked at a clearing where she hoped she would find the vegetables. As she walked and looked at the spot ahead she felt a sharp stinging as something hit her left leg. The pain was intense and immediate. She felt the calf muscle begin to tighten up in response.

Pulling back the leaves she looked. A drop of blood ran down her calf, but she didn't see what had hit her leg. The wound burned and stung intensely, causing her eyes to water. Gritting her teeth, she turned away from the clearing and went back to the path. She was only a few yards into the jungle near the grove. By the time she got onto the trail in the grove she was limping noticeably.

When she got back to her cave, her strength barely holding on, she all but collapsed to sitting outside the cave leaning against the wall. Sweat soaked her shirt and poured off her face unnoticed as she fought to get breath into her lungs. Whimpers escaped her throat with each rasping breath and pulses of pain shot up from her leg through her entire body.

It felt like forever, though she knew only minutes had passed, before her breathing calmed and the pulses of pain receded enough to be tolerable. Carefully she shifted and scooted across the ground to reach the spring. The cool water rinsed the sweat off her face and neck as she almost cried. The tears pooled in her eyes as fears raced through her mind. She knew if she couldn't walk, she would die here. She couldn't die here, somehow she had to survive and get back home. The tears fell and she couldn't stop them. Fear kept her trembling and crying as keenly as she felt the pain from her leg.

The tears receded, leaving her feeling exhausted. She wasn't dead yet, and she wasn't going to give up. She didn't care if Frank was anywhere near, she pulled her damp shirt off and rinsed it off in the spring. With the wet shirt in hand she got back to her feet, keeping her weight on her right leg. The left hurt like hell, but it supported her weight. It was enough for her to get into her cave and lay down. In moments she was restlessly asleep.

On wakening she saw that it was clearly late afternoon. The pain from her leg seemed tolerable. She sat up and inspected her leg. There was not much blood from the wound, just a few drops leaving reddish brown trails on her calf. The skin was red and itching around what appeared to be a small puncture wound. It looked like she had been hit by either a single fang or a thorn. She couldn't recall plants with thorns when it happened, so she chose to think of it as a bite.

Looking at her things she saw she had two pieces of fruit left in her cave, the grumbling in her stomach clearly indicated she had not eaten in several hours. While grabbing the fruit she spotted a small plastic box sitting among her things. The small first aid kit sat unopened from the day she first arrived. Feeling some relief she grabbed it, a dry t-shirt, and made her way back out of her cave to the spring.

The cool water provided some relief from the burning and itching as it washed the dried blood away. The puncture didn't look as bad once it was clean, and the ointment in the first aid kit reduced the burning.

Pushing worries out of her mind, she put her dry shirt on, ate the fruit she had and went back to lay down and rest. Hopefully by morning her leg would feel better, because she didn't have any food. She didn't have a choice but to go out in the morning to get something.

The bite on her leg kept itching like crazy. It kept her awake into the night. Now she felt a pounding headache caused by lack of sleep. She worried that it could be something worse than just lack of sleep. Her entire body felt so weak and lethargic that every step was an effort that threatened to drain her willpower. She would have to deal with those things though, even if all she wanted to do was to lay back down and try to sleep and hope her leg would quit itching. She had learned early on that without a refrigerator to store food, she had to go out every day to gather something to eat or go hungry. The nights of going hungry were not the least bit fun, and she didn't look forward to another one.

She wished this was happening to Frank instead. She knew the thought was unfair, and she didn't care. Everything she was doing was a struggle, while he seemed to get by so easily. He probably would have done something to fix his leg within minutes of getting stung. He probably would have killed whatever it was and cooked it for dinner.

On wobbly legs, she went down the trail that led to the fruit trees. The idea of trying to catch fish or crabs for lunch or dinner sent waves of nausea through her stomach. She was walking toward the grove to get some fruit so she would have at least a little something to get her through the day. She stopped and leaned against a tree with her head swimming and her vision blurred. She realized now that she felt much worse than she had let herself believe. The bark of the tree slid against her palm as her legs gave away. She didn't even know she was falling. She only knew in that moment that something was really wrong. The hard packed sandy ground bruised her arm when she fell on it. She was unconscious before her head hit the base of the tree, leaving a bloody gash on her forehead.

She barely opened her eyes, it felt like she used all her strength just to open them a crack. There was something yellow and fuzzy swimming in her sight and something warm and wet pressing against her lips, then liquid on her tongue. She swallowed, drinking in whatever it was. Her eyes closed again, taking the fuzzy yellow thing from her sight.

She was sitting up. Her body was wracked with aches, and her head was hurting so much she couldn't bear to think. She felt something press against her lips. Keeping her eyes closed, she opened her mouth enough to feel cool water slip onto her parched tongue. The water was the only thing that felt good. She swallowed, letting it cool her throat and body as it went to her empty stomach.

She managed to drink only a few mouthfuls before slipping back into unconsciousness.

She lay still on the pallet letting her eyes remain closed for at least another moment. She didn't want to wake up because her body felt so tired. She was awake though. She knew she was awake and that her mind was not going to go back to sleep. Her entire body felt sore and her head was hurting. She opened her eyes slowly to see the rocky roof of the cave. She stared at it a moment before she realized it was not her cave. The ceiling was larger than the ceiling of her cave. Did that mean she was in Frank's cave?

It hurt to move, but she made herself roll onto her side so she could look at the cave before she got up. It was definitely his cave. This was the first time she had been in this cave, but she recognized the signs that someone lived here. There was a small pile of folded clothes near the pallet. She recognized her shirt sitting on top of her shorts.

She took in a slow breath, her ribs felt sore as she did. She knew she was sick. She felt it through her body. She remembered feeling sick, but needed to get something to eat, but after that her memories became strange and disoriented. The vague memories of pain, yellow lights, and drinking something were there, but at the same time just out of reach. She just couldn't remember them clearly.

The thought of food made her realize she was hungry, but she didn't want to eat at the same time. She also realized that her throat was dry and her tongue felt like it was sticking to the inside of her mouth. Despite how thirsty she felt, she didn't want to move, or try to get up.

She heard him just before he entered the cave and looked to the entrance. He was carrying one of his fishing spears and looked at her as he entered. The moment he realized she was awake, he set the spear down and came straight to her. He reached out to place his fingers on her forehead, then her cheek.

His fingers felt cool and refreshing on her skin. It felt nice just to be touched. It was Frank though. She couldn't trust him after all the things he had said. She heard him let out his breath like he was sighing. Was that a relieved sigh? It was so hard to think straight. He pulled his hand from her head and shifted to pick up a crudely made clay pitcher and cup. He poured some water into the cup. The sight and sound of the water reminded Michelle of just how thirsty she felt. Michelle tried to lift herself to sit up, but her arm refused to work right, or just refused to pick up on her own weight.

He noticed and set the cup down. He sat down on the pallet near her head and gently helped her sit up leaning against him. His skin felt cool against her bare back, but he felt warm at the same time. Holding and supporting her, he brought the cup of water up to her lips and held it while she drank. Her throat was so dry it was hard to swallow, but she did. The water felt wonderful. She closed her eyes as she let the liquid slip down to her stomach. She stopped after a few sips to just breath and let her body just lean against him. She knew that she was too weak to do anything but lean on him, it was more in her mind than her body that she let herself lean on him.

"You need to drink it all." he said softly.

She opened her eyes in surprise. Except for Christmas, he had not spoken anything to her in a soft or gentle tone of voice. The hatred and scorn she had grown accustomed to was not there.

He placed the cup against her lips again and she drank. As she drank she realized how thirsty she really was and drank as quickly as she could swallow. The cup emptied after only a few swallows. She wanted more to drink. She felt she needed more to drink. Somehow he balanced the cup on his lap and grabbed the pitcher to fill it again without letting her slip out of his embrace. She couldn't bring herself to thank him, but she was grateful he didn't let go. She felt so weak she was sure she couldn't hold herself up. She drank the water he offered her and two more full cups before her stomach felt too full to drink more.

He gently laid her back down on the pallet. She realized she had not spoken a word to him since he came and gave her the water. Part of her did not want to lay down. Mostly she knew she didn't have a choice. She looked at him. Really looked at him. He looked tired, and his brow was creased with worry lines. She didn't know how long she had been living on this Island with him and he refused to help her, yet now she was lying helpless in his bed and he was caring for her.

"Have I been here long?" She whispered. She remembered waking up not feeling well and trying to go get something to eat.

"Four days," he replied in the same soft voice.

The answer should have shocked her, but she knew he was telling the truth. She could feel it in her body. "What happened?" She could feel her throat drying again, but now that she was talking, she felt the need to know.

"Try not to speak. You're dehydrated. I will tell you as much as I know, but I need to make sure you don't get sick again. You understand?"

She nodded. She didn't want to speak with her throat feeling sore and dry.

> Save me now before my world falls
> Save me now from myself
> Before the dawn
> Save me now I'm at the reaper's door
> Can't you see, you hold the key
> To set my mind free
> - Save Me From Myself by Sirenia

"I found you on the trail to the grove, unconscious and bleeding…"

In the early afternoon, Frank headed toward the grove to pick a fresh lime and other fruit to go with the fish he caught that morning. He saw Michelle lying in the path well before he got there. He didn't rush to her. He still wished she was not here. One day he wakes up on this island, then later he finds he is sharing it with someone he wished to never see again.

When he got to her, he saw the blood on the ground. In that moment, he felt concerned. He had wished her to hurt so many times. Now she was hurt and he couldn't bear the thought, the hatred was pushed out of his heart and fear came in to take its place. He reached down to shake her…

"You were hot, feverish. I tried to wake you, but you didn't respond…"

Her skin was dry and burning to touch. He shook her shoulder and called her name, but she did not respond. Her eyelids didn't flutter, and she didn't utter a word. The gash on her forehead looked terrible.

"I carried you back here…"

He scooped her up, cradling her in his arms. She was like a rag doll and hard to hold. It took some maneuvering, but he finally got her head to lean on his shoulder and held her close so that she wouldn't slip. Her entire body was burning with fever. He could feel it radiating from her in waves. He swallowed against the lump forming in his throat. She was in serious trouble, and he was stuck on this island with very little to help her. "God please don't let her die", he thought as he turned to carry her back to his cave.

Every step strained his arms and back as he worked to keep her from slipping. Her body remained limp and unresponsive, leaving him with the task of doing everything to keep her held up in his arms.

He sat down to rest before attempting to carry her up the last hill to his cave. He was breathing hard, both from the exertion and from a surge of nervous adrenaline that he wouldn't be able to help her. As he sat there catching his breath and resting his muscles, he heard her breathing. The sound sent a shudder of relief through his body. He fought to keep the tears at bay. "Just hang on please. I don't want to see another death. Please just live." He whispered to the unconscious woman in his arms.

His body wanted to rest more, but he couldn't. She was still alive, and she needed help right now. Struggling, he stood up with her in his arms. The last hill awaited. The hardest part of this trip, and he would do everything he could to see that she survived.

"You didn't wake or stir the entire time I carried you. You didn't react when I laid you on the pallet."

The muscles in his back protested as he laid her down on the pallet in his cave. He wanted to sit down or lay down and just rest, just catch his breath and let his shaking muscles have a break. That would have to wait though. He grabbed a clay pitcher and went deeper into the cave where he had found a spring of cool water. It formed a small pool that drained into the rocks at the same rate it filled. It was a continuous source of water and it was refreshingly cooler than the streams outside the cave.

The fever felt much too high. He had to do whatever he could to cool her. He pulled her shirt off and placed wet rags under her arms. He used a washcloth to clean the blood off her forehead and face. Once clean, the gash on her forehead didn't look as bad. It was still bleeding slowly, but it wasn't as deep as he had feared it would be. It was still bad enough to make his stomach queasy. He hated the sight of blood and wounds, there was no time for that now though because she needed help right now. He swallowed, trying to force his stomach to settle down so he could focus on figuring out what she needed. He finished washing off her face and the wound on her head, rinsed the washcloth and left it on her forehead hoping to reduce her fever.

He placed his blanket over her to cover her nakedness. There was one plant he had found that be used as a salve on cuts. There was one other plant that produced a cottony fiber that should work as gauze if he needed to cover the wound on her head to stop the bleeding. It wasn't a short walk to get to the plants. He was going to have to risk it though.

"I didn't want to leave you alone, but I didn't have a choice. I had to find something for your fever and the cut on your forehead…"

It was early evening when he returned to his cave. She did not look as though she had stirred at all while he was out. He pulled the cloth off her forehead, it was mostly dry. She was still feverish, but the bleeding had stopped. He applied the greenish salve to her forehead. He knew it must have hurt when he touched the wound, but she didn't even flinch.

Cautiously, he used his fingertips to place water on her lips. He knew she would have to drink something or the fever would dehydrate her beyond his help. The water slipped between her lips, she seemed to stir, and swallowed. It might have been involuntary, but that didn't matter. As carefully as he could, he kept applying drops of water to her lips, letting them drip into her mouth slowly. He ignored the growling of his stomach as he focused and getting as much fluid into her as he could manage without risking it getting into her lungs. He knew she had not gotten enough, but it seemed like she relaxed. Her breathing became a little easier for a moment, and she stopped swallowing the drops of water.

He resisted putting his hand against her skin again. He knew she was still feverish. Resigned, he got up and went outside the cave to fix something to eat. The fish he caught that morning had waited all day to be cooked. It would have been lunch, but he realized now that he had skipped lunch completely. It was amazing what worry could do to a person's mind and body.

As he cooked, his mind drifted and gave thought to how he would feed her. If she didn't wake up, no, he couldn't even let himself think that. She would wake, and he would make sure she got enough to eat to get her back on her feet. Then she could go back to her own cave. He had some smoked pork left, and there were ripe beans in the garden. Those should work to make a broth. Some beef or chicken would be better, but he knew he was far more than fortunate to have as much as he did. He looked back into the cave. He could barely see her due to the shadows caused by the setting sun and the fire. He wished he had a lantern or a flashlight, but wishing wasn't going to help. If wishes could help, then he would wish she was in a hospital, or that they were both back home and healthy. As near as he could tell, she had not moved. The broth would wait for tomorrow then. He may have food, but he couldn't waste it.

His mind kept going back to her as he ate. He didn't even taste the fish and green leaves he had gotten for his dinner. He cleaned his clay plate with his mind barely on his tasks. He had seen death before. He watched his wife Mary die. It took almost five years before her body just couldn't keep fighting. Every day of those five years was like watching her die. The memories taught him a lot, but Mary didn't have fevers, and she didn't lay unconscious and unresponsive until that last night.

He shuddered as that last memory ran through his mind. He felt the lump in his throat and tears burned his eyes. He grabbed one of his crudely made cups and went back into the cave. He lifted Michelle's upper body and braced her against his body. He filled the cup with water from the container and brought it to her lips. As he did so, he whispered into her hair, begging her to drink some water and to get better.

Somehow she did drink. She drank half the cup of water. He felt cool tears running down his cheeks as relief flooded through his body. He laid her back down. If only he had something for her fever. One of those plants out there probably contained something that would reduce her fever, but he had no idea which plant could possibly help.

A yawn pulled his mind back to the moment. He felt the soreness as his back continued to protest carrying her back to his cave. It wasn't going to be an easy night. He went to his belongings and grabbed a spare blanket. She had the only comfortable sleeping spot in the cave. It was big enough for both of them, but he didn't feel comfortable to sleep next to her. Despite his worry for her health, there was still too much that had happened between them. He couldn't lay with her.

He stepped outside the cave hoping that it wouldn't rain.

"I had to clean you the next morning. I guess I should have anticipated that would happen. I had been through it before, but I still didn't think about it…"

His back protested every move as he woke the next morning. It hurt enough he wondered if it would be worth it to try and get up. He slept on the only level spot of ground he could find close to his cave, but he was pretty sure it had more small rocks than any other place he could have slept. Staying there laying on the ground just wasn't possible though. He meant to get fruit yesterday for last night's dinner and this morning's breakfast, but finding Michelle unconscious on the path interrupted those plans.

Once he thought of her, he pushed through the pain and got up to go check on her. The urine smell hit before he entered the cave and grew increasingly stronger as he went in. Frustration hit him as strongly as the smell did. Why didn't he think to remember her body would still work, even if she was completely unconscious. He had to gather food, and every bit as important, he needed to clean her and the bedding.

Keeping his mouth and nose covered, he put his hand on her forehead, she was still feverish. Her skin was dryer than the day before. Her breathing sounded slightly labored, but she was breathing. With a mental groan, he gathered the small container and got up to go fill it with fresh water. It was the only thing he had he could use as a bucket. It wasn't much, but it was going to have to do.

The blanket was soiled, so Frank threw it outside the cave, or at least he intended to throw it outside the cave, some of it actually landed outside, but the rest stopped just inside the cave mouth. The denim of her shorts was soaked through, as well as the sand under her. He didn't have a choice, she had to be cleaned or she would develop a bad rash in addition to the current problems.

He had seen her naked before, but that seemed a lifetime ago and everything was different now. It really shouldn't be a big deal, but inside his heart he couldn't quite tell himself it wasn't a big deal. Despite the circumstance, the sound of her zipper still carried an intimacy about it. Maybe it was just the sound a zipper made; whatever it was, it was enough to push him into feeling more uncomfortable than he already felt. The wet fabric resisted coming off her hips, and resisted as much moving down her legs.

"I think something had bitten you. There was a knot on your left calf that was very red, and hotter still than the rest of you…"

The swelling around the knot and the feverishness of it was intense. He imagined it hurt intensely even with his light touches. The center of the swelling was white with pus just under the skin. As carefully as possible, he worked the soiled shorts over the swelling, avoiding the skin as much as possible. There was so much to be done, but he could only do one thing at a time. The first was to clean her as best he could. He threw the shorts and panties, both landed well outside the cave.

He used the washcloth, pouring water onto it to rinse it often, and cleaned her skin as much as he could. If he could have carried her, he would take her to the pools not too far away, but between his back, her weight, and how treacherous that trail could be, he wasn't going to risk it. It wasn't much different than cleaning a baby after changing the diaper; she was just bigger, and clearly more mature.

He had only one towel. There was no choice but to use it. He laid it on the opposite side of Michelle. Once he had cleaned her front to the best of his ability, he rolled her over onto the towel and finished cleaning her from behind.

The soiled sand was going to be even more of challenge. He wasn't going to use his only water bucket to carry it out of the cave. It took a few minutes to find a section of bark that was big enough to carry enough sand to make it worth the effort. With a smaller piece of bark to scoop the sand, Frank returned to the cave and removed the soiled sand. He only had to dig down a couple inches to remove it all.

He checked on her periodically as he worked. Nothing was changed. She was still feverish and not responding. His concern continued to grow as he worked. He ignored the rumblings in his stomach. Finding something to eat just wasn't as important at the moment. He knew that would change though, he couldn't ignore his own health and put her at even more risk by not being able to help her.

He brought fresh sand in to replace the sand removed. Then went to wash off with the clean water that pooled up further back in the cave. He repositioned Michelle so that she was laying on her side as comfortable as he could manage. The knot on her calf looked awful now that he had her turned where he could get more light on it. There was definitely something under the skin causing the swelling and fever in her leg. He decided he was going to have to find what it was and get it out.

He pulled out his knife and took it out to his fire pit. It took a few minutes of coaxing to get the coals to light the tender. It had to be done. This was the only way he could sterilize his knife before he used it on her leg. He picked up a burning stick and held the flame to the blade until the handle grew warm to the touch. It was as clean as he could make it.

When he returned though, he realized he didn't have anything clean to cover the wound with. Sighing, he picked up the make shift bucket with the wash cloth and carried them to the fire. He set the knife and washcloth down on a rock by the fire and emptied the water out off to the side. He made two trips to gather enough water to fill the hollowed stone he used for boiling water and sometimes cooking. All he could do now is wait for the water to boil. He checked on her, she was still laying where he left her, then gathered the blanket and clothes. There was a waterfall and small pond not far from his cave. A place where he could rinse out the clothing. There would be enough time for even the blanket to dry before nightfall.

"I don't know why I didn't think to see if you had an extra blanket in your cave. I guess I was so scared that you weren't going to make it that I wasn't thinking straight…"

When he returned with the clothes. The water was boiling. He put the washcloth in the boiling water, then left it to take the blanket and clothes to hang on branches to dry. He checked his watch. He wanted the washcloth to boil at least fifteen minutes.

He knew he couldn't delay it any longer. If he waited too long, he wouldn't have enough light to see her leg clearly. The washcloth had boiled for more than the fifteen minutes he wanted. He pulled another branch from the fire to sterilize the knife again. Used a cooking stick to get the washcloth out of the boiling water and returned to the cave. He left the washcloth hanging from the stick so it could cool and maybe even dry out some.

He picked up her leg and put it across his lap. As carefully as he could, using just the tip of the knife, Frank cut the skin across the knot. Pus and blood streamed out as he cut. He could smell the infection. Thick, white pus came out in one lump. It was like acne, only something worse. She didn't even stir as he cut. He knew it had to hurt. There was too much pressure and infection for this not to be hurting her intensely.

He set the knife aside, keeping the blade off the ground. He squeezed as gently as he could. More blood and pus came out of the wound. Then surprisingly it was followed by something so dark it seemed black. It was oddly shaped, and probably as long as his thumbnail. He pulled it free from the wound. It was soft and mushy though he expected it would be hard, like a thorn. He set it aside on a rock to look at it later. He squeezed again, being as careful as he could. Nothing but blood and yellowish pus came out of the wound. He grabbed the washcloth and cleaned her leg off, getting as much of the pus away from the wound as he could. He set the leg down and went to get his only clean shirt to cover the wound. It wasn't much of a bandage, but it would have to do.

"I never could figure out what the black stuff was that was in your leg. I burned it that night instead of keeping it around…."

He sat back against the side of the cave. He felt a need to rest for just a moment. He couldn't see anything else he could do for her, yet he knew he would have to do more. She lay still as he sat there looking at her, wondering if there was anything else he could do. Worrying that he hadn't done enough. The rumbling in his stomach pulled his thoughts back. Reminding him that he had to take care of himself so he would be able to take care of her. Every day on this island was a day of survival. A day that he had to find something to eat, and a day he had to take care of his shelter. Now he wasn't just taking care of himself though.

He went out of the cave and emptied the boiled water, rinsed out the make shift pot, and refilled it with water, adding beans and smoked pork. Leaving it to simmer. Frank left to gather more food.

Between the cave and the ponds were some vegetable plants, the same plants where he found the beans. Down below, past Michelle's cave was a grove with fruit trees, and some pineapple plants. He wasn't used to gathering so much. He knew he would need extra if he could get her to eat something. He didn't have time for fishing today, hopefully tomorrow would be a better day. He returned with the fruits and vegetables to find the beans simmering. The water had turned into a nice broth which would be perfect if she could drink some of it.

"It had only been a few hours since I removed that thing from your leg. But you seemed so much better. I wasn't sure, but I thought you were breathing easier and your fever had come down some. You managed to drink a few sips of broth and water…."

She was definitely getting better. The next morning she did not have the fever she had run for the last two days. She seemed more like she was asleep than unconscious. The worry and fear he had faced since finding her began to ease up. He spent the morning fishing, catching one more fish than he normally would. He gathered more fruits and vegetables in the afternoon. Each time he returned to the cave, he stopped in to make her drink at least a few sips of water. That night she managed to drink some broth made from the fish caught that morning.

She remained unconscious through the next day, but she continued to look better and he was able to get her to drink more water and broth. By late evening she seemed more like a person sleeping than one in a coma.

The next morning she woke up.

"I had just returned from fishing and was coming to check on you when I noticed you were awake. I can't begin to describe the relief I felt. In that moment, I wanted to cry, but I held my tears in check…"

> I'm holding on your rope
> Got me ten feet off the ground
> And I'm hearing what you say
> But I just can't make a sound
> - Apologize by One Republic

Michelle could feel the soreness penetrating all of her muscles. Frank's voice was soothing, threatening to relax her back to sleep. She felt like she needed to pee though, and she didn't want to fall back to sleep. After sleeping for four days, she wanted to stay awake. She wanted to be better, and go back to taking care of herself.

The last thought gave her the motivation to try. She could tell his story was finished for now. He might have more to tell her later. She wasn't sure she wanted to hear more though. The certainty that she would cry if he told her more gave her reason to move. She pushed against the ground, trying to lift her body. Her arms felt so weak, it took everything she had just to try. She felt his hand under her shoulder supporting her, but not lifting. She managed a few inches off above the ground before her strength gave out. He held her right there, keeping her secure and steady while her arms trembled underneath her. She tried to keep the tears away, but she couldn't stop them in the face of how weak she felt, how unable to do something so simple. He gently lowered her back to the pallet, "you will be ok, you just need some time to recover."

Between sobs, she responded, "I need to pee though." Thoughts of sleep had fled her mind after the exertion of trying to even sit up. Without a word, he helped her turn over and slipped his arms under her; one arm under her legs and the other under her back. With the blanket held in place so it covered her, he began lifting.

"What are you doing?" she tried to protest.

"I'm taking you out so you can go pee." he replied in a matter of fact way.

She tried to push against his chest. "God! No Frank. Please. I can do this. You don't have to do anything more."

He held her tighter, she could feel the tightness of his muscles in his arms and chest, as he settled back on his knees. "Michelle."

She gave up trying to push against him for the moment. It was clear she didn't have the strength to stop him from picking her up like a small child. "What?" She responded weakly.

"Shut up." He said sternly. The command in his voice was clear. She couldn't even think of anything to say, or find her voice to speak. It was like her own father had just told her to be quiet until he gave her permission to speak. She tried to look at him, to gage the expression on his face, but he stood and she found her head pressed against his shoulder, held there by his chin. Without another word from either of them, he carried her out of the cave and into the waning sunlight. She did what she could to hold onto him and make it easier and used her other hand to weakly hold the blanket against her body. She obeyed his command to stay quiet and let him carry her, and despite her trembling muscles, she made herself help him.

He carried her downhill and into a group of trees. She could hear a stream gurgling through the stand of trees. The sound of the water brought back vague memories of her first day when she spent hours searching for fresh water. He lowered and sat her on a log. When she felt the smooth bark on her bare skin she became very aware that she was naked under the blanket. She mentally thanked him for bringing the blanket to keep her covered. She considered telling him thank you, but she felt she wasn't supposed to speak yet. It was like she needed him to speak first and give her permission to talk again.

He shifted until he was in front of her. His hands kept her steady on the log as he did so. While facing her, he lifted her slightly and moved her back until she felt her bottom move past the back of the log, and back further until she felt another log behind her. She realized he had set this up like a toilet seat. He took her right hand and set it on a sturdy branch beside her. "You can use this when you are done." He said as he pointed toward some cottony wadding pushed into the V formed by a branch that grew from the log.

She didn't think she would be able to pee with him sitting there watching her. As this thought crossed her mind, he turned away while still squatting in front of her. He kept her left hand held securely on his shoulder. She understood his unspoken implication that he was staying right there for her, while trying to give her privacy as well.

Between the branch and his sitting still and patient, she felt secure enough to sit on the logs. She closed her eyes and let her body relax so she could pee. It took a moment, but the muscles finally released. It burned, but she felt relief at the same time. It was only a short time and she was done. He held her left arm tighter as he felt her shifting to get the cottony wadding to clean herself. The blanket had all but fallen to her feet, held up between her knee and his back.

She felt her heart pounding in her chest, and her vision grew dark as she worked to keep herself steady. She didn't even notice he was helping her until his arms were holding her steady again. The dizziness passed, leaving her feeling slightly nauseated. "I think I should lay back down." She whispered against his chest. She felt him nod as he repositioned her so he could pick her up again.

The trip back up the hill was a daze. She barely held on to him as he carried her back to his cave. When they reached the top of the hill, her heart beat had stopped pounding in her chest. She could feel his heart beating in his chest though. She knew he was exerting himself to carry her like this, but she knew she couldn't help him. She used up all the strength she had just to hold herself steady while peeing.

She thought his arms trembled as he lowered her onto the pallet. She wanted to hold onto him to keep herself steady just a moment longer, but her arm slipped off his neck without any resistance. She wanted to say something, to tell him thank you, or just hear his voice, but the thought faded away from her mind as she slipped back into sleep.

> Everytime I try to fly
> I fall without my wings
> I feel so small
> I guess I need you…
> - Everytime by Britney Spears

When Michelle awoke, the cave was bright with morning light. She knew she was still in Frank's cave. She felt a brief stab of jealousy that the area around his cave got so much more sunlight than her cave did. More than that though, she realized she felt better than the night before, except for the intense pressure from her bladder.

She pushed to sit up, a slight wave of dizziness hit, but she pushed through it until her upper body was upright. When she started to pull her legs under her though, a sharp stabbing pain from her left calf struck her so hard she felt like her entire body had been hit.

She didn't realize she had laid back down or that she had cried out until she felt Frank holding her arm. Sweat and tears were falling off her face as she caught her breath. Blessedly, he didn't say anything. He simply sat there holding her hand and arm to let her know he was there. As her breathing came under control she said the first thing that came to mind knowing he was sitting there watching her. "I'm a mess." Her voice was hoarse, but not as bad as yesterday.

"Yep." he stated flatly. There might have been humor in his voice, but she didn't catch it right away.

Her bladder reminded her why she tried to get up in the first place. She was glad she hadn't peed on herself, as bad as her leg hurt, that wouldn't have surprised her. "I need to pee." She told him. "Really bad."

"I guess that's why you tried to get up then." he said as he shifted onto his knees. In moments he had one arm under her legs and the other under her shoulders. She reached up and put her arm around his neck, gladly accepting his help. He carried her just like he did yesterday, except this time she was fully awake and willing him to go faster and wanting to cuss him every time he hit a bump or jostled her. She felt those very intensely in her bladder and in her left leg. She didn't remember the leg hurting yesterday, but she didn't remember much about yesterday at all. Maybe he could tell her what was wrong with her left leg, or maybe he already did and she forgot.

Oh God why couldn't he go faster, her bladder felt like it was going to burst. The sound of running water was not helping at all. The trees looked vaguely familiar, and why was he stopping now? The answer came quickly enough as he lowered her to the branches where she could sit like she was on a real toilet. Albeit a toilet covered in smooth bark, but still she could sit.

She realized she was sitting over a stream, so she didn't even have to worry about covering it up with dirt after she was done. Frank had definitely found a good idea with this one. He held her arms and helped her get situated, then turned away while still holding her left hand on his shoulder. Clearly he was still worried about her. The thought had barely crossed her mind when her bladder released. The relief was so intense she felt blackness blurring her vision momentarily. She shifted and felt the pain in her leg again and immediately stopped moving. Frank squeezed her hand, keeping her steady as her body continued to relieve itself.

Finally, after what seemed forever, her bladder was empty. "Frank, do you have something I can use…"

"It's just to your right." he pointed without looking.

She saw the cotton wadding and remembered it from yesterday. She pulled some free, cleaned herself and let it fall to the stream below. She pulled the blanket back up to cover herself while he waited patiently in front of her.

Once modestly covered again she cleared her throat. He turned and helped her back into his arms. The trip back up the hill to his cave was much easier than the trip down. Her leg still complained with every bump, but the pain was reduced to a throbbing ache. She stayed quiet, keeping focused on holding onto him.

He was breathing harder by the time he topped the hill, but his arms kept her firmly held up. He was definitely much stronger now than when they parted. Back then he could pick her up, but actually carrying her somewhere would have been a challenge. Now he had done it two days in a row, and up a small hill as well. His biceps were very tight against her back and legs. Feeling his muscles against her like that almost made her forget the pain in her leg.

As he lowered her down in the cave she realized he was sweating as much as she had earlier. "Now you're a mess." She observed.

He exhaled noticeably as he sat back. "Yeah, I guess so." He managed to say as he was catching his breath. "I'll get us some water so we can wash up after the sun is higher. I need to go get us something to eat first."

Her first thought was to help, instead of letting him do all the work, but the throbbing in her leg told it wasn't going to be possible for her to move on her own. She looked at the scrap of cloth wrapped around her calf, it was probably from one of the shirts Frank never seemed to wear. "What happened to my leg?"

He looked at her, his eyes curious. "I guess you don't remember what I told you yesterday. I should have realized how tired you were."

The memories of the day before did come back. It was like a trickle, and what she remembered seemed hazy and distant, but it was there. "I guess I remember some. It's all kind of fuzzy right now."

He looked thoughtful and paused before he spoke again. "I guess I'll worry about getting us something to eat then. We can talk later if you want and I'll tell you again if you don't remember. Before I go though, let me look at your leg."

"I would like to know what happened. I remember something was wrong, it was itching and bothering me." She said as she sat still for him to remove the piece of cloth wrapped around her calf.

The wound was on the outside of her left calf and she could clearly see why her leg was hurting. The cut on her leg looked terrible. How did she not notice it before? He calmly looked it over, then wiped off her leg around the edges of the cut. Each brush of cloth stung to the point of tears. She bit her lip and held them in check though, so that he could finish without distraction. His ministrations took far too long, but mercifully were over soon enough. He got up and went to the other side of the cave and returned with a bowl, another strip of cloth, and what appeared to be a spiny plant stalk.

He broke the plant and pushed some pulp into the bowl. He used his thumb like a mortar and crushed the pulp in the bowl. The crushed pulp was soothing as he gently applied it on her leg. Then just as gently he wrapped her leg in the fresh strip of cloth. Despite how gentle he was, her leg still hurt. The throbbing was more intense, yet somehow not as bad at the same time. Giving into the pain for a moment, she laid back and stared at the ceiling, trying to focus on anything other than the pain.

"Are you ok?" his voice was filled with concern.

She answered in a whisper, "I'll be ok."

"That's the first time I took care of your leg with you awake."

"You did fine. It was already hurting before you took off the bandage." She said with the same whispery voice.

The expression on his face indicated he wasn't convinced, but he didn't say anything in response.

"Really Frank. I'm ok. Thank you."

"I guess I don't need to tell you to stay here then." he said, recognizing her white lie. He pulled out another strip of cloth and moved the bowl of crushed pulp within her reach. "In case you need them. I'll be back in a couple hours."

She didn't try to get up, choosing instead to lay on her back and look at the ceiling. The noises he made as he gathered his gear were comforting. Those sounds pushed away the loneliness she felt almost every day. They pushed away the fear of being alone and helpless. She was helpless, but she wasn't alone. She knew that if he had not found her, there was a real possibility she would have died. She pushed that thought away before she started to cry. Maybe after he went out, but not yet. If she cried, he might delay going out, and she couldn't keep him here when they both needed to eat.

She felt and heard her stomach grumble as soon as that thought crossed her mind. She sighed. Realizing she would have to wait for him to return before she could eat something. The ceiling of the cave stayed in her sight, though she wasn't really looking at it. It was just a rocky roof that was secure enough they could stay in here for shelter. With a mental effort, she focused on a shadowed spot almost directly over her. In conjunction, she focused on her breathing and relaxing so she could push thoughts of hunger out of her mind.

The exercises were interrupted by Frank coming back and setting something at her side. "I'm sorry. I should have brought you this sooner."

She looked over to see that he had placed a bowl with ripe fruit within reach. She didn't know if she should hug him or just cry with relief. She chose something in between and whispered, "Thank you."

"I'll hurry back," he mumbled, and headed out of the cave.

She ate the fruit he gave her, her stomach stopped grumbling. With nothing else she could do, she laid back and returned to looking at the ceiling. Within minutes of focusing on her breathing she was asleep.

She awoke from the nap before Frank returned. Daylight had warmed up the area around the cave, leaving her feeling sticky and generally yucky. Her calf wasn't hurting as much as it did in the morning. As carefully as she could manage, she maneuvered herself into a sitting position.

Pain shot through her calf as she pulled herself up, but it didn't get as bad as it did earlier. The skin around the edges of the makeshift bandage felt normal when she touched it. She was afraid she would find the skin hot with infection, and felt immense relief when she touched the skin and it felt normal. It was very tender to the touch. She pressed with her fingertips, exploring where it hurt and how much pressure caused it to hurt.

The light touches became a gentle massage as she worked to sooth the aching muscle. Massaging the muscle made her realize just how tight it had gotten. She thought back to the night before when he told her what had happened. She didn't want to depend on her memory, but she was sure he said she was unconscious for four days. That would definitely explain why her muscles were tight and sore. She needed to move and exercise all of her body, but she couldn't do that until the wound on her leg healed enough to support her weight.

She closed her eyes as her fingers moved to her right calf and continued the massage on her sore muscles. He told her what happened while she was unconscious, but the memories of what he said seemed so hazy. She let her mind relax, not focusing on any thoughts or trying to force her mind to remember. In her relaxed mind she was barely aware of her fingertips gently massaging her right calf. The sound of the surf reached her ears. She could barely hear it inside the cave. Once again she felt a brief twinge of jealousy. She never heard it from inside her cave. The jealousy didn't stay though, she didn't let any thoughts stay. Instead she let them come and go without conscious effort. The relaxation efforts paid off as the fragmented memories of last night began to come together in her mind. She let the pieces of memories come together slowly, as if she was watching a movie in her own mind.

At times it wasn't easy to stay mentally and emotionally relaxed. She recalled in his words how close she came to dying here. When he described what he found in her leg, she understood that he did what was necessary. If it had not been for him and his help, she wouldn't have survived.

As the memories of Frank's story came to a conclusion, she let her body and mind come up out of the induced relaxed state. Normally when she used this relaxation technique she came out of it and felt refreshed. This time she felt tired and sleepy. He was still out, so she laid back down, pulled his blanket up to cover her nakedness, closed her eyes and fell back to sleep.

> I had to be free, had to be free
> It's all that I wanted
> I wanted to see, wanted to be
> Alone if I needed
> - Free by Sarah Brightman

The sound of Frank, outside the cave, greeted her when she woke up. It was much warmer, and she had pushed the blanket off. It was probably later in the afternoon, judging by the angle of sunlight entering the cave.

The sound of wood cracking as he chopped it for the fire was comforting. She recalled the countless hours of finding sticks small enough she could break on her own. She knew how much she struggled to keep her fire going. The flint she arrived with was nearly worn out, at the rate she was going she probably wouldn't have a fire in about two months. In part she felt guilty that she wasn't helping, but mostly she felt glad and relieved that she didn't have to worry about that burden. That sound was also a good indication that Frank was successful in catching something to eat.

Carefully she rolled onto her side, stretching sore muscles in her back as she did so. Slowly she finished rolling over onto her stomach. She stretched out and heard her back pop in three places as she did. It was almost as loud as the noise he was making outside, but it felt so good as she sighed and exhaled from her stretch. She pushed her arms out over her head, feeling sand press into the palms as she stretched. Muscles protested with longing to be up and moving as she stretched. The feelings extended into her mind and emotions. She wanted to be out there helping him by picking up the wood as he chopped it, or better yet back at her own cave working to gather wood for her own fire. Wood for a fire pit she knew was cold and lifeless right now. She wanted to walk the trails finding her own food, exploring this island that for now was her home.

Despite the discomfort from her leg, she sat up again, determined to learn the limit of her mobility. The muscles in her left leg felt weak and lethargic; a dramatic contrast to the muscles throughout the rest of her body which wanted to move and exercise. As she shifted, she felt the need to pee again. The timing made her sigh with exasperation. The idea of making her way down to the bathroom was so daunting she felt her heart sinking at the very thought.

If she continued to try and move, her bladder would protest even more, but laying back down would leave her muscles frustrated with lack of activity. Closing her eyes, she did all she could to push thoughts of needing to pee out of her mind, as if forcing her body to believe she didn't need to. In the back of her mind, she was sure it wasn't going to work, but that wasn't going to stop her from trying.

She didn't realize she no longer heard him chopping wood until he cleared his throat. Relief filled her face as she opened her eyes to see him standing in the entrance of the cave. The desire to jump up into his arms swept through her powerfully. It wasn't a sexual desire, simply the knowledge that he was the means for her to get relief that she desperately needed. Reaching up to him, her eyes pleaded for him to help her up to go pee. As he stepped forward she noticed the stick in his hand. It was about as long as one of the fishing spears, but much thicker.

He set it down and took her hand. "Do you want to try to stand?" He asked in a voice filled with tenderness and concern.

"I need to pee again." The words sounded so crass as she heard them return to her ears, but it was a simple truth.

He acknowledged with a nod and pulled her up seemingly without effort. Spikes of pain shot through her left leg as she tried to put some weight on it. With a gasp she shifted her weight to her right leg as he quickly steadied her and pulled even more of her weight off her legs. She felt her fingers digging into the taught muscles of his forearms as the pain began to recede. He felt so solid and strong under her hands. He was here and he could take care of her. It was what she needed right now, and she emotionally let go of the need to fight him.

She looked up, blinking away the tears that watered her eyes from the pain. It was tolerable again. A brief smile formed on her lips to let him know she was ok again. She caught the look of fear in his eyes before it softened to relief. He reached down to scoop up her legs, swiftly picking her up into his arms. She felt his biceps tight against her back and legs as she put her arm around his neck and rested her head against his shoulder and neck. She was safely in the arms of this man who was strong enough and willing to take care of her during her time of need. It was enough and she relaxed into that feeling. She didn't care whether or not it would last in that moment. All that mattered was that he was here and holding her.

The walk to the restroom, it was the only way she could think of it, seemed to last only seconds. All those other times the walk here seemed to take forever. She knew it had to do with her emotions and that she had let go and accepted him taking care of her, and still that thought didn't bother her. Somehow he managed to lower her so that her right foot touched the ground first. Slowly he let her take more and more of her weight, while she grabbed a branch with her left hand to help with balance.

Carefully she maneuvered her body into position on the toilet he had put together. He stayed close in case she needed help. Looking at her pale skin as she sat there, two distinct thoughts crossed her mind. The first is that she probably should have put on some clothes before she came down here, and the second was that she really wanted a bath or a shower. The latter wasn't a reality, but she could at least get a wash cloth and wash off so that she would feel less grimy, sticky, and probably would smell better too. She knew the days of being in his cave had to have left her smelling pretty ripe.

She completed her business and looked up to see that he was standing a few feet away clearly not looking at her while she relieved herself. She couldn't help but smile with gratitude for him being so conscious of her privacy. While using the cottony material to clean herself off she became very aware that she was not wearing anything and he was about to pick her and carry her again. The only choice she had was to try and walk back up the hill on her own, and she knew her left leg was not going to hold her up for that trip.

She covered herself as best she could before clearing her throat and speaking, "I'm done."

He returned to help her up. If he noticed her shyness, he didn't indicate anything, just gently took her into his arms again and picked her up. His bare chest felt hot against her side, and his muscles were again tight against her. His skin felt so good, and somehow he smelled clean but very much like the man he was. His musky scent filled her nose in a very intoxicating way, and why did she have to be completely naked right now? Sex just wasn't possible with him having to take care of both of them, and it wasn't that long ago he made it clear he didn't want to have sex.

Relief flooded her mind as they entered the shadowy cave. She didn't want to let go of him, but he couldn't carry her forever. She also didn't think asking him to lay down with her was an option either. Somehow she had to convince her body to remember that he was a man from her past, not a man in her future. That was something she knew clearly in her mind and heart, but her body had its own ideas and those ideas including getting him as naked as she was. She remembered he was very well endowed and that was a thought she needed to get out of her mind very quickly. Once back on the ground, she pulled the blanket over her naked body, wishing it could cover her thoughts as much as it covered her nakedness. She tried to focus on the dull aching pain throbbing in her left leg, but even it wasn't doing much to calm her thoughts.

He grabbed the stick she saw earlier so that he could show it to her. She didn't want to take her eyes off his bare chest, but somehow she did and what she saw captured her thoughts and pushed the idea of sex out of her mind for the moment at least. He had fashioned a crutch for her. The top was covered with leaves and she saw the cotton wadding in the seams of the leaves. Speechless she reached out and caressed the wood before taking it into her hand. She didn't even notice the blanket slip down as she looked at the crutch in her hands. At home a doctor could have given her one and it would have just been a tool she was forced to use until she got better. Right now it represented a measure of freedom, and he had done something special just for her. He really was doing what he could to take care of her, and this crutch was so much more than she expected.

"Thank you," she said with a whisper.

"You're welcome," he responded equally quiet. "I imagine you would like to wash up and get dressed again."

She couldn't help but look at him with gratitude. Remembering that she had thought those very thoughts only a few minutes ago made her wonder if he had read her mind or if he was intuitive about her needs. "God, you have no idea how much I would like that."

He smiled, "then let's see how this crutch works. The sun is up and warm, the perfect time to wash up."

She smiled in return, held the crutch in her left hand and gave him her right hand. He lifted her up firmly, keeping her steady with a hand on her back. Despite the years since the last time she used a crutch, she managed to get it under her arm. It was maybe an inch too tall, but it was definitely close enough she could manage with it. He kept a firm hold on her right hand as she took her first step with the crutch.

In spite of him being in the way more than helping and trying to remember how to use a crutch, she somehow got outside the cave. The joy of being on her feet had her smiling the whole way. Even though being upright was making her left leg hurt, it didn't matter, she was really back on her feet and could do something more than lay on her back waiting for Frank to wait on her or help her.

He led her to the spot where he washed the dishes. Three large bowls, two pitchers, a washcloth and towel were already waiting for them. Once there, he helped her sit on the bare rock. In moments the first pitcher of water washed over her as he poured it out over her hair and body. She washed with the washcloth, being extra careful on her left leg. He took the washcloth and washed off her back. In minutes all of the water was emptied from the bowls and pitchers, and she was happily drying off with the towel. It was amazing how quickly one felt better after a refreshing bath or shower.

As she dried off, he stepped away and returned with her clothes. Gratefully she accepted the clothes and his help in getting dressed. All over she felt refreshed and better than she had felt since before something had bitten or stung her leg. In fact, this was probably the best she had felt since Christmas.

He helped patiently as she practiced using the crutch. Within the hour she was able to hobble around the campsite with only minor difficulty. He turned his attention to fixing their meal as she learned how to get around and also to be able to sit without falling over. The workout made the muscles in her right leg burn, and the crutch caused her armpit to feel sore, but it was all worth it. It felt so good to be up and about. Maybe tomorrow she would try to figure out how to do a happy dance with the crutch.

She sat near the fire pit enjoying the scent of the fish roasting over the fire and eating a few nuts and berries while the fish cooked. He had refilled the bowls and washed off also, the towel and wash cloth hung out to dry. She felt bad about leaving him a wet towel to dry with, but he didn't complain. The sun and air dried his skin as he worked on their dinner. The roasted fish filled her stomach very nicely. It was the first real meal she had eaten in several days and her body felt happy inside.

With the setting of the sun, tiredness returned to her body, she knew she was still healing and didn't have the energy she used to have. With him following, she made her way down the hill to use the restroom on her own. She did need some help getting back up the hill, but she knew as her strength returned she would manage the trip on her own and not need his help.

She laid down on the blanket to sleep and watched as he left. She didn't think to ask where he was going. She just laid back and closed her eyes and fell asleep within minutes.

> You know that I want you
> And you know that I need you
> I want a bad, bad romance
> I want your love and I want your revenge
> You and me could write a bad romance
> I want your love and all your lover's revenge
> You and me could write a bad romance
> - Bad Romance by Lady Gaga

The following morning he was there when she woke up. He helped her get on her feet, but let her walk on her own to go use the restroom. She nearly celebrated the victory of getting back to the cave without needing his help to get back up the hill. She sat down by the fire pit to catch her breath and he gave her fruit for breakfast. He grabbed his knife and fishing gear, leaving her sitting there with her victory.

After resting she began working on making herself more useful around camp. The things he had done for her the past few days were beyond measure. How could she ever repay him for saving her life? She really owed him a great debt just because she knew she could still return to see her children, her family, her friends, and her home again. In that moment she would do anything she could possibly do for him. No matter how small, and as long as it was something she was capable of doing, she would see it done.

Without the use of her left leg, she was hindered in being as helpful as she wanted, but she did the best she could getting the dishes washed off. Luckily he had left behind two pitchers of water. She needed one for drinking water, but the other went to keeping things clean. She kept a small fire going so they wouldn't have to worry about that when he returned.

Her skill with the crutch improved with each step. The movement seemed to increase the strength in her body until she almost felt normal again. Once again it felt like a small victory, and she was going to take every victory. At midday she ate a small meal of fruit, berries and nuts. She found the pouch of dried pork, but felt self-conscious taking something she knew he had worked hard on.

He returned to find that she had kept busy doing what she could for the camp. She insisted on taking the large fish from him to clean it and prepare it for dinner. He accepted and allowed her to work on the fish and went to chop wood for the fire. It seemed like a daily exercise for him. The wood pile had enough on it to last them at least three days, but he went to chop more. He definitely intended to stay prepared. On the plus side, if they ever spotted a boat or plane, it would allow them to build a large fire and improve their chances of rescue. That by itself made his efforts worth the time.

How he managed to drag the large logs uphill amazed her though. He seemed even stronger now than when she first saw him on this island. It was no wonder his muscles had grown so firm. The soft man she once knew had become something very strong, very firm, and she couldn't deny the thought that he was beautiful to look at. Still she didn't consider everything changed between them. He made no moves to be anything more than her caregiver. He invested his time in taking care of her, something which deserved a huge amount of appreciation.

The remainder of the day they passed their time much the same as the day before. He filled the bowls and pitchers with water and they both washed up. They roasted the fish for dinner relaxed as dusk set in and turned in for the night.

The next morning she tested some weight on her left leg. It hurt, but she was able to put a small amount of weight on it. The feel of her foot on the ground improved her balance and made it possible for her to use her right hand with more freedom as she walked. Frank went out to gather more fruit and brought back crab for dinner. While she worked on preparing the crab for dinner he disappeared for about an hour. She had the crab in boiling water when he returned carrying what appeared to be a pair of zucchini. She eagerly sliced them up and roasted them to go with dinner.

The area around the front of the cave was becoming neater and more organized due to her efforts to help. He showed her the spring further into the cave where he filled the pitchers and bowls with water. She wasn't sure if she could manage filling them on her own yet, but at least she knew where to get the water from when she felt she was strong enough to do so.

She could get around the area without assistance from him, and she was taking advantage of that as best she could. She longed to get back out on the trails and seeing more than just this area around his cave though. She knew she was getting cabin fever from being stuck in one location for so long. Thinking about it, she realized she had been here a week. Four days of that week were spent unconscious, but still it was a week. Tomorrow she resolved to get away from the camp site to do some exploring.

The left calf was hurting and sore when she woke. Despite the pain she got up and got started on the day. Frank joined her by the fire pit as they sat and quietly ate their breakfast fruit. The moment felt so comfortable, no words were necessary. Hopefully he felt the same. Neither rushed to finish breakfast, somehow they both felt lethargic at the same time, as if their bodies wanted to take a day to rest. If only they could afford that luxury. They couldn't though, it didn't matter how either of them felt, every day they had to get up and do what was necessary to survive.

As if echoing her thoughts, he stretched, sighed with resignation and got up to get his fishing gear. He didn't need to say that he would return shortly, but he said it anyway. She mumbled something equally non-committal in response before he headed down the trail. As much as she wanted to go back into the cave and lay down, she wasn't going to let him do all the work while she did nothing. She got up and set about the task of taking care of the camp.

Filling the pitchers and bowls with water was time consuming because she couldn't carry them, she did manage to fill them and scoot them along the ground a step at a time to bring them all back out. The wood was piled and ready for the fire, so she didn't need to do anything with that, and she didn't bother to put any in the fire pit to start the fire. It just didn't seem necessary. She cleaned the dishes and stacked them neatly on the cutting table.

She hoped moving around and taking care of the camp would loosen up her leg, but it didn't help. Luckily it didn't become worse either. It just remained sore and seemingly more lethargic than she felt in the rest of her body.

Everything she could do in the camp was done and Frank was still out fishing and gathering their next meal. The sun was rising up to its zenith. Without anything else to do, she gave in to her desire to return to the cave and lay down. Maybe a bit of rest would get her out of the lethargic funk she woke up with. She stared at the ceiling until her eyes closed with sleep.

When she opened her eyes again, she realized she felt decidedly better. The soreness in her leg was back to what she now considered normal. A fish, gutted and scaled sat on the cutting table waiting to be cooked for their evening meal. She didn't see or hear Frank anywhere nearby and it was still early in the afternoon.

She still wanted to get out of the camp, get away from the cave, even for just a short time so that she wouldn't feel so trapped here. Since her leg felt sore this morning, she decided not to go down the hill to either her cave or the beach. The trail to the restroom ended at the restroom, and she went there without any problems, that left going back to the side of the mountain and seeing if that trail went past the point where it went up to the viewpoint she saw at Christmas. She wasn't going to attempt to climb up to look at the cove, the idea was pleasant, but she wasn't going to test her leg on those rocks.

Getting a few feet out of the camp improved her mood, just seeing something different was enough to make her feel she was getting away. The trail was as easy to follow as the one down the hill that went past her cave. It seemed strange for such trails to be here when there were only two people on the island. Maybe Frank had been here long enough to form the trails. The trail below led between the beach and the grove, with a side trail to the wall that separated them from the wild pigs.

That thought raised her curiosity about where this trail would lead. She paused at the spot that led up to the lookout point, looking up and remembering how beautiful the cove looked. She still didn't feel comfortable to try and climb up there though, so she turned her attention back on the trail in front of her. It became rockier, but it still looked passable, even with the crutch under her arm.

The right side of the trail remained a rocky wall leading up the side of the mountain and the left side sloped downward gently. Ahead she saw the ground on the left side rise up to level with the trail. That gave her something to walk toward, a place where she could explore something new on the island.

The level ground was filled with trees and shrubs. She saw what appeared to be narrow trails leading in, and areas through the trees where there were fewer trees. The trail continued alongside the mountain wall. She considered whether or not to follow one of the narrow trails to see what was in the jungle, but she wasn't sure how well she could maneuver her crutch and really didn't like that she couldn't see all of the trail. The idea of getting bitten or stung again made up her mind to not get off the trail.

She turned and continued to follow the trail. As she moved clear of the level area on her left and the ground slowly began to slope down again. She noted a large rock protruding from the right ahead. She couldn't tell if the trail ended there or not, so she continued to walk there to see what she would find.

The trail grew narrow and continued around the rock protrusion. The ground sloped down sharply at this point, creating what could be a dangerous spot to fall. She heard the clear sound of a small waterfall. It sounded like it was just around the curve of the rock protrusion she stood at. If she were to take a guess, she would say this trail led to that waterfall. She looked at the trail judging whether or not she could safely cross it. It looked wide enough for her to safely plant the crutch with each step, so she decided to take the chance.

The ground was solid under her feet and crutch, and she kept her right hand on the rock beside her. Carefully and cautiously she stepped along the trail, watching each step to make sure she didn't slip down the slope into the shrubs and trees below. The sound of the waterfall grew clearer as she moved around the rock. As she came around she saw a clear pool, rippling from what she was sure were the effects of the waterfall she didn't see quite yet. The water ahead looked cool and inviting, making her wish she had brought a towel with her. Of course she didn't know she would find a pool of water she could take a dip in, or she would have brought the towel. The pool was barely large enough to swim in, she spotted a small waterfall cascading about four feet off a rock into the pool. Above that she saw another waterfall falling onto rocks or another pool before the water fell into the pool she saw before her.

As she moved around more she spotted a towel hanging from a branch of a tree growing close to the rock she had her hand on. The trail moved away from the rock slightly so that it went between the tree and the pool. A few steps more and she spotted Frank standing under yet another waterfall. He had his back to her as the water crashed over his head, washing through his hair and down his clearly naked body.

With a start she realized his right hand was in front of his body and moving rhythmically. His left hand against the rock wall in front of him, holding him steady as he masturbated under the water fall. The muscles of his back and buttocks shook as he stroked. The sight sent a flush of heat through her cheeks, and she felt her loins tighten and throb as lust raced through her body unexpectedly. She gripped the crutch tightly in response, and could not take her eyes away from the man in front of her pleasuring himself under the waterfall.

Finally she had proof that he did still feel lust. She hoped right now he was thinking of her. She was the only woman available on the island. The idea of him imagining having sex with her as he masturbated sent more thrills through her body. She felt her wetness against her shorts as she watched and felt an orgasm building. Her right hand remained touching the rock wall and her left gripped the crutch. Without touching herself in any way, she felt the orgasm building as surely as she knew his orgasm was building. His shoulders grew more tense and she could tell that his strokes were moving faster.

His entire body tensed up and he turned his face up into the water as his orgasm hit. With it she felt her own orgasm shudder through her body. It wasn't as intense as his orgasm in front of her, but she felt it thoroughly from head to toe and barely kept her balance on the crutch. She gasped with the pleasure as the waves of her orgasm subsided with his. He turned around and leaned back against the rock wall, the water falling down his front, his eyes closed in relief and pleasure.

Slowly she backed up, not wanting him to know that she had just watched him. This was his private moment and she had spied on him. The trembling in her legs and the wonderful feelings washing through her body didn't complain about what she had done though. He was definitely worth watching. In seconds he was hidden from view and she carefully turned around to make her way back to camp.

Once around the rock she moved as quickly as her feet and crutch would carry her. Every step she worried he would catch up to her and know that she had spied on him masturbating. She felt little jabs of pain in her left calf with each step, but she didn't slow down her pace. She couldn't bear the embarrassment of him catching up to her.

She arrived back at the camp with her heart pounding and sweat beading on her brow. She sat down to rest and looked back to see if she could see any sign of him on the trail. He didn't appear, and slowly her breathing came back under control. She got up and grabbed the wash cloth off the branch it hung from and quickly washed off her face and neck. The cool water refreshed and calmed her.

She recalled watching him and felt her body respond again. She thought about going into the cave to touch herself to get some relief, but pushed the idea aside, she didn't know how much longer it would be before he returned and she didn't want to get caught masturbating in his cave. She splashed more water onto her face to try and cool down.

Somehow she managed to get herself under a semblance of control. He returned carrying his towel and some vegetables to go with their dinner. The sight of his bare chest brought back the memories of him fully naked. She turned away before lust took over again. She knew she wanted to go pull those shorts off and see him completely naked again, and she knew she was not going to consider turning those thoughts into actions.

Blessedly he didn't notice that she was acting different. He hung up his towel and grabbed a few sticks of wood to get the fire going. As he did so, she noticed the position of the sun and realized it was late afternoon. She had no idea how long she had napped, or how long she was away from camp. She did know she wanted to go back to that waterfall to get a shower and maybe relax in the pool of water. In fact, that idea sounded good enough for her to consider going right now, but then she would have to reveal to Frank that she knew about the existence of both.

She grabbed the crutch and pulled herself to her feet. She couldn't let him do all the work for dinner and she desperately needed to get her mind off sex that she knew was not going to happen. It felt so good to feel so alive again. She didn't know how many months she had gone without thinking about sex or feeling any desire for sex. She did know she hadn't gone that long without thinking about sex since she hit puberty. She also knew she was very close to this being the longest she had gone without sex since losing her virginity.

She went into the cave where he kept the few herbs he had found and gathered. It seemed like so little, but even a small amount did wonders for the flavor of the fish. The idea of going back to eating bland fish didn't seem appetizing. She rubbed the dry herbs into the fish and set it back on the cutting table to await cooking.

She avoided looking directly at Frank, and somehow she made it through dinner and the rest of the day without tearing his clothes off. She watched as he took his blanket and headed away from the cave. It took every fiber of her strength to not call out to him to come back and stay in the cave with her. She didn't even know where he went to sleep. Just that he left, giving her the privacy of his cave while he went elsewhere.

She laid back to look at the ceiling, knowing that she wasn't the least bit sleepy. The quarter moon provided some light outside the cave, but not enough to really see. The trees and bushes formed into vague formless lumps of shadow. Darkness filled the cave, leaving her unable to see the ceiling or anything else more than a foot or two away. The only sound she could hear was the muted crashing of waves. A sound that reminded her of the cascading waterfall.

She gave into those thoughts and memories. In moments she was back standing near the waterfall watching Frank standing under the water. She could remember the details of his muscular back, the strong legs and the shape of his ass. The way the water ran down his sun browned skin was beautiful to her sight. In her fantasy she didn't stand there watching, she undressed, feeling the cool misty air on her body. She dropped the crutch before she reached him, limping the last two steps. He turned to her, quickly taking her in his arms, the heat of his hardness pressed into her stomach.

She gasped with pleasure as his lips met her own, his tongue pushed into her mouth. With strong arms he lifted her off her feet, turning both of them until he pressed her back against the smooth rock wall. Water fells over both of them in sheets and waves as she pulled her legs up around his waist. He slid into her, filling her.

The orgasm hit her so hard she could barely hold onto the fantasy. She felt her own wetness coating her fingers as she touched herself for pleasure. The cave echoed her gasps and muffled moans until she stifled them. Breathing rapidly through her nose she tried to listen for any indication that he may have heard her. As her breathing returned to normal she heard nothing but the muted crashing waves. She relaxed, feeling her body relax with the glow of pleasure. She still wished he was here beside her, but the feeling of pleasure could not be denied. She closed her eyes and drifted off to sleep still thinking about him.

> I told myself I won't miss you
> But I remembered what it feels like beside you
> I really miss your hair in my face
> And the way your innocence tastes
> And I think you should know this
> You deserve much better than me
> - Better Than Me by Hinder

When she woke in the morning, she didn't want to get up, and tried to will her body to go back to sleep. She thought it might work until Frank came into the cave trying to be quiet. He actually was pretty quiet, but just feeling his presence was enough to push sleep away for the morning.

"I'm awake." She whispered, to let him know he didn't have to try to be so quiet.

"I'm sorry, I didn't mean to wake you." He whispered back.

The sound of his voice and his thoughtful words brought a smile to her lips. He didn't notice as he was bent over picking up clothes. "I've been meaning to ask. Do you mind if I go into your cave to get you a change of clothes?"

She blinked as the implications of what he said sunk in. The entire time she had been up here, he hadn't gone to her cave for any of her things. In part she wished he had gone to get her things, having them up here where she could reach them would be nicer than not knowing whether or not her things were still safe. Yet what he did was very respectful.

"Of course, please, I would like to know my things are ok."

He nodded in response and carried the clothing out of the cave. "Do you feel well enough to take a longer walk today?" He asked as he came back into the cave.

She thought about the hill that led back down to her cave. She could probably get down the hill and to her cave, but she wasn't sure her leg could handle coming back up. She was going to have to try it and soon, but another few days of healing surely wouldn't hurt. "I don't think I can make it back up the hill and I don't want you to have to carry me up that hill again."

He glanced out the cave in the direction of the hill, then turned his attention back to her. "I didn't mean to go down the hill. It's Saturday, and I normally wash my clothes and blankets on Saturday. I found a good spot for washing, and I think you can make the walk if you feel up to it. I thought you would like to wash your own things too."

She felt her face flush and swallowed against her suddenly dry throat. He was talking about the waterfall and the pools. The memory of seeing him yesterday returned to her mind clearly. "I can try." She managed to whisper. Hopefully he didn't hear the tremble she knew had to be in her voice.

"Great. Is there anything in particular you want me to get for you?"

The temptation to tell him to get everything was huge in her heart. Something in her held back though. "My blanket, towel, and my change of clothes please."

"No problem, I'll go get them now, it's best to take care of washing in the morning so everything has time to dry."

She watched as he got up and left the cave again. Watching him walk away she felt a longing to get up and go with him. That longing didn't seem to understand that she felt pain in her left calf though, or that it didn't fully support her weight. Still, it would have been nice to just get up and go with him, to see her own cave and see her own things where she left them. That wasn't going to happen though and she knew it, so she pulled the blanket off and grabbed her shorts. Pulling them on, she brushed the never ending sand away as best she could. The sand didn't irritate her the way it first did, it was simply a fact of life now.

Since she couldn't sleep, she decided to start her day. She found the fruit he had gathered, there was extra for them for tomorrow, which showed that he planned ahead. She took and ate what she needed, then brought the blanket out to add to the small pile of clothes outside the cave. There was no indication of what else he wanted or needed, and she didn't have anything else to do to take care of the camp, so she sat down on the rocks by the fire pit and waited for him to return. She listened to the various birds calling out to each other in the surrounding trees. She couldn't see any of them, but they made their presence known. She picked up a stick and doodled in the sand and ashes while waiting for his return.

She was almost to the point of writing in the sand when she heard him coming up the hill. He carried her blanket with her things wrapped inside of it, and she recognized her black bikini in his other hand. The bikini had sat at the back of her cave where she put it the day she moved into the cave. She didn't know if the beach was safe for swimming, and she didn't have time to go lay out on the beach to work on her tan.

"We should wash the shirt and shorts you are wearing too." He said as he handed her the bikini.

He was right. All of her clothes needed to be washed. She used the small pool by her cave to wash off, but it didn't hold enough water to wash her clothes. The only time any of her clothes had been cleaned was when he cleaned them while she lay unconscious in his cave.

"Thank you. Should I change here?" She said while pulling herself up on her crutch.

"You can change in the cave. I'll wait out here for you."

With that he began gathering all the clothes and blankets into one blanket for carrying. She hobbled into the cave and quickly changed into the bikini, coming out minutes later to find him waiting by the clothes with his back to the cave. Despite how many times he had seen her naked and his own admission that he cleaned her while she lay unconscious he didn't intrude on her while she changed. Why did it matter so much to him that he not intrude like that? After yesterday's events, she wouldn't have complained. At the moment she could easily imagine boldly undressing for him, but without any way of knowing if he would respond with the lust she wanted, she couldn't give into that thought.

She dropped her clothes onto the pile with the others, and watched as he closed up the blanket around them. He pulled the bundle up over his shoulder with ease and turned to walk the trail to the waterfall. Without hesitation she followed. He walked slowly, allowing her to follow without struggling to keep up. He seemed to know how fast she could go, and maintained the pace along the trail.

When they reached the stone that forced the trail to curve out next to the steep drop he set the clothes down and turned around. "This part can be dangerous. I'll guide you first, then come back for the clothes."

"I trust you." She responded. She knew she could safely navigate this part, but she didn't want to let him know that she had already been here.

He moved backwards, carefully setting each foot down and watching the trail. He kept his right hand close to her left shoulder without touching. She kept her right hand on the stone and watched carefully where she put the crutch and followed him slowly. She moved slower than she did the day before, letting him guide her and set the pace. She knew she could get around the rock faster, but he was walking backwards and needed to be extra careful.

About half way around the rock he asked a question that made her stop in shock. "Did you make it this far when you came out here?"

Flustered with the realization that he probably caught her spying despite her best efforts to not get caught, she stammered, "What? What do you mean? What are you asking?"

He smiled, "you've already been here. Sometime in the last couple days I think. I saw the tracks from your crutch yesterday. I was wondering if you made it this far and saw the waterfall too."

With a herculean effort, she pushed her fear back enough so she could answer him. "Yeah, I made it this far." She didn't return his smile as easily. The pounding of her heart as she thought about him catching her made it hard to breath. She took another step, and he resumed leading her around the rock. She wanted to say something to throw him off, but knew that anything she said could cause him to realize the truth of when she did follow the trail and see the waterfall.

Her heart rate almost felt normal when they got past the rock to where the trail became safe for her to walk without him worrying again. Still he led her to the tree that stood between the rock and the pool. "We should leave your crutch here. I don't think it would be a good idea to let the wood get wet. I'll carry you to the upper pool. That's where I'll wash the clothes."

"That probably isn't necessary," she protested.

He turned around and looked around across the pool where the smaller water fall fell into it. The fall was at least four feet from its top to where it fell into the water below. "Yeah, I'm sure, I know your leg is supporting some of your weight, but I don't think you can climb up to that pool right now. She followed his eyes and she couldn't argue with him. She couldn't even see how to get across to climb up that small wall. Was the upper pool just out of sight over that wall, or did they need to climb more.

Resigned, she dropped the crutch by the tree, "Ok." She didn't want to say anything else and the tone of her voice carried the frustration of having to be carried again. He squatted down in front of her so she could climb onto his back. At least he wasn't going to carry her like he did before. Somehow she knew that being that close to his chest, feeling his heartbeat and his muscles might be more temptation than she could resist.

Wrapping her arms around his neck and her legs around his waist, he lifted her up easily. She felt the hot skin of his bare back rub against her stomach and breasts in a very tantalizing way, and realized that with her legs wrapped around him the temptation was coming on very strongly.

He grabbed her legs to add support and walked directly to the waterfall, but turned and crossed an apparently shallow part of the pool. The cascading water misted her skin with refreshingly cool water as they passed the first water fall. She smiled and turned her face to the mist, letting it distract her from how good he felt against her.

When they got to the wall he told her, "Hang on, so I can use my hands." She felt him release her legs and gripped him tighter to keep from slipping. She could see another pool of water over his shoulder, and another waterfall feeding that pool. The air felt warmer, but she knew that might be because she wasn't under the mist from the first waterfall. He grabbed the top of the wall, found a toe hold and pulled both of them up. The flat rock at the top of the wall was covered with mostly dry sand that slowly descended into the clear water of the pool before her.

He stopped at the top of the wall on his hands and knees, "Ok, I think you can make it from here."

Reluctantly she released her grip and gently slid off his back. The pool of water was several feet across and despite the ripples caused by the water fall it was clear enough to see the clean sandy bottom. She almost hated the idea of getting in the water just thinking about how much of a mess she knew she really was.

"Don't go near the waterfall over there," he said as he pointed at the waterfall that fed the pool. "The water is pretty warm there, give your body a chance to adjust first."

The waterfall was several feet away across the pool. She didn't think she would have any problem following his advice.

"Let me see your leg." He pointed at her left calf.

She stretched her leg out for him. In part she wanted to turn away as he removed the wrapping. Every time he did she wanted to turn away, but her curiosity held her each time and she watched as the wrapping came away and the wound came into view. The skin was nearly sealed and it barely bled any longer. Each time the wrapping came away cleaner, today there were only a couple of dime sized spots on the wrapping.

"You can get in the water. I'll go get the laundry."

She nodded in response, not trusting her voice at the moment. She wanted his hands back on her leg and more. If she said anything, she was sure he would know how much she wanted him. She was almost to the point that she wanted to reach out and take him instead of waiting for him to make a move. The only thing that held her back was the memories of his anger, and the way he rebuffed her at Christmas.

He left while she sat there restraining her hands from reaching out to him again. Once he was across the first pool she began sliding carefully into the upper pool.

When her feet hit the water, she realized the water was warm, very warm. It was way too warm for water falling down in a stream off the mountain. Thoughts of wanting fled from her mind as she climbed into the warm soothing water. It was the luxury of a warm bath, something she had not enjoyed in months.

When he returned with the laundry, she was already in the water immersed up to her neck. She could have stayed here for hours without complaint. She didn't even open her eyes as she heard and felt him move past her. Curiosity took hold and she opened her eyes. He was sitting on a rock beside the waterfall readying to wash the clothes they had brought. He didn't look at her or acknowledge her. It seemed he decided to let her soak in the water and take care of the laundry himself. She couldn't let that happen, thus she crawled through the water to where he sat. He looked up at her approach, but remained quiet.

She decided not to speak either, but grabbed one of her shirts from the pile of laundry and pulled it into the water with her. He used the rock and the waterfall to scrub and rinse the laundry one article at a time. She worked with him, finding another rock in the water to scrub the clothes. The process was time consuming but relaxing. As they finished a group of clothes, Frank took them back to the trail and hung them from branches. Their laundry soon filled the trees to dry, and he returned from taking the last trip to join her relaxing in the water.

Words were not needed, he just sat down in the water until it was up to his neck, leaving a respectful distance between them. The water was enough for her in that moment as she sank down to her neck and closed her eyes. She felt clean. The water soaked away months of dirt, sand, sweat, and even tears. Keeping her eyes closed she let her head sink below the water and soak into her hair. She held her breath as long as was comfortable before coming back up to let the water rinse her hair. Strands of wet hair brushed her shoulders. Hair that was at least three inches longer than it was the day she arrived, and it felt clean.

Frank got up out of the water first, climbing down the wall and getting under the first waterfall. His shorts clung to him like faded denim skin. She looked at her hands and saw they were white and wrinkled from sitting in the water for so long. She needed to get out too. The water was so wonderful she didn't want to leave, but she knew she was going to come back to this no matter what he had to say about it. He didn't own the Island, or even his own cave. He could get angry about it if he wanted, but as long as she was stuck here, she was going to take advantage of this amazing spot.

She got out of the water and carefully made her way to sit on the wall with her feet hanging down. The pain in her leg was so diminished she felt she could stand on it, but didn't want to take the risk.

He reached up, putting his hands under her arms and gently lowered her to her feet. He kept most of her weight on his own arms. In that moment she looked into his eyes. The piercing green gaze looked back into her own. She couldn't read that gaze though. Did he still hate her, or was he ready to accept her and work with her to survive on this island? She tried so hard to see something in his eyes, but she either couldn't read him, or she couldn't trust her own mind to read what she saw.

He pulled his gaze away and moved to her left, acting as her crutch and guiding her to the waterfall. The water was cool on her skin, like a quick shock that quickly woke up her senses. It washed through her hair and down her skin, rinsing off all the hot water and sand leaving her refreshed, awake, and alive.

Still acting as her crutch he took her to a flat area of ground to lay down and let the sun dry her skin. The moment reminded her of the trip she took to Mexico where she had the chance to spend time relaxing on the beach. She took the trip alone, drinking in the solitude and the chance to get away from so much overwhelming stress building up. The memories of why she felt stressed didn't cross her mind, it was just the same feeling. Today she once again felt a measure of peace and relaxed with the sun soaking into her skin. Today she let go of fears and worries and just relaxed, the same way she did on a beach in Mexico. The only thing missing was a cool fruity drink. She could wish all she wanted, but she wasn't going to have everything.

Time didn't have meaning, and it passed quickly. It seemed they had barely been there, yet been there for too long when she heard him get up and begin gathering the laundry. It didn't matter how much she didn't want to let go of the peaceful feeling, she wasn't going to let him do everything all the time. Getting to her feet wasn't too difficult as she remembered to keep her weight on her right leg and keep her balance. Once there it was an awkward ungainly hop/limp back to the tree to retrieve the crutch. The left leg barely hurt and she considered testing her weight on it, but the thought of getting around the rock reminded her that she needed to be cautious still. There was plenty of time to test its strength back at camp.

As she leaned on the crutch she realized he already had all their clothes sitting on top of one of the blankets, ready to be folded up to carry it all back. He took care to place it all in neatly to minimize wrinkling. He didn't need to worry about that with each of their shorts, but she couldn't help but smile at his consideration for her shirts.

"Let's get you around this rock, and I'll come back for this," he spoke while standing up.

She nodded and followed him. He walked backwards, lightly holding her right forearm and she lightly rested her hand on his. She could feel the tense readiness in the muscles of his arm. He truly was ready to catch her if she slipped. If he tried, they could both end up falling down the steep bank into the rocks and trees below. The thought of both of them laying there too hurt to do anything made her shiver and pause.

He paused with her. "Are you ok?" The concern in his voice couldn't be masked. They were only about half way around the rock.

"Yeah, I probably shouldn't have looked down. Give me just a moment."

He stood there holding her arm gently, making his presence known. She heard the buzzing of flying insects as they stood there quietly until he broke the silence. "What were you doing when you got that bite on your leg?"

Startled by his question, she looked up at him. His green eyes looked directly into her eyes, piercing into her with his gaze. "I was trying to find the vegetable plants. I wanted something more to eat than fish, crab, and fruit." The words seem to tear through her throat.

"Where?" His face remained calm, and she realized what he was doing. He was distracting her, she could see it in his expression and hear it in his voice. He was right of course, she needed to stop thinking about what could happen and stay focused on getting around this rock to a safer place.

"I went off the trail just past the grove. I thought I saw a clear area and I wanted to see what grew there." She answered his question first. "I'm ok now, can we get past this rock please?"

He nodded, checked his footing and began moving backwards, guiding her again. She focused on her footing and each step she took, knowing that every step was one step closer to the next goal. The hand on her forearm seemed to transfer strength into her as she felt better with each step until they were soon walking at an almost normal pace considering the circumstances. The trail moved past the rock and the steep decline. She moved closer to the rock wall and without a word sat down with the wall to her back. "See, I told you I was ok," she said to Frank in response to the look of concern he gave her.

He smiled at her levity. "Yes, you are ok. I'll go get our laundry." Despite the smile, the look of concern didn't truly leave his eyes. He touched her knee briefly as he stood up and returned for their clothes and blankets.

She sat still resting her head in her hands and focused on breathing and calming her heart rate. She knew it wasn't the fear of falling that made her panic. It was the fear of Frank getting hurt. It was the fear of being responsible for him getting hurt. The thought of pulling him down with her sent that fear through her and put them both at risk. She didn't understand that feeling or why it happened when it did. She knew this trail now, and should not have had trouble crossing it.

The pounding in her heart subsided, and breathing became easier before he returned. He was safe and for now he would remain safe. She pulled on her crutch to get back onto her feet, ready to return to camp with him. She saw his free hand begin to reach out to her, but he stopped himself. She sensed he was ready to help her to her feet, but stopped himself so that she could do it on her own. He couldn't always be there to pick her up and they both knew that was the reality.

With a quiet nod he turned and began walking back to camp with the bundled up clothes thrown over his shoulder. She followed easily, putting more weight on her left leg than on the crutch. The pain was barely noticeable, but she could tell the muscles still needed more time to regain their strength. At camp he took all their clothes to various branches and hung them to finish drying. She followed along and helped as best as she could. He put up three clothing items to each one she managed, but at least she did something.

When you gonna make up your mind
When you gonna love you as much as I do
When you gonna make up your mind
'Cause things are gonna change so fast
- Winter by Tori Amos

    They took the time to eat fruit and nuts he had gathered and saved up for days like today when he didn't have time to hunt and gather. The sun was still high in the sky as they finished their small lunch. She wondered what other plans he had for the day. "I have one more thing to show you," he spoke as if he just read her mind. He got back to his feet and she followed. He went back to the trail heading to the waterfall. He couldn't mean the lookout spot, she had already seen that, and she didn't think she could climb up there with the crutch. He passed by the rocks where they climbed up to the lookout point without a pause. At least she didn't have to worry about trying to climb those rocks for whatever he wanted to show her.

    Where the ground leveled out on the left side of the trail he turned and went into the brush. She recalled this spot the first time she passed by here. It looked like a trail into the brush to a clear area ahead, the spot she avoided the first time she passed by here. The idea of something lurking in that brush kept her from thinking of going through that area, but he didn't hesitate until he noticed she wasn't following. "It's ok, I've been through here lots of times. It's safe."

    She looked at the trail, his legs hidden by the brush below, and followed. He turned and led on to the clearing. When they got there, she saw that it wasn't a true clearing, just that the plants were shorter in this area. They looked different here. She started to look closer when she saw him squat and pull the leaves aside on one of the plants. Whatever he was looking for he didn't find, and moved on to another plant. She leaned on the crutch and watched. Her jaw dropped when she saw him pull out what looked like a zucchini.

This was where he found the vegetables. He shared the secret with her. These were garden plants. How did they get here? Why here on this Island? The questions filtered through her mind as she went to the closest plant to see what she could find. She could barely contain her excitement going from plant to plant. When she spotted the herbs she almost squealed with delight.

"What did you find?" His words interrupted her thoughts and excitement. "You made an excited noise," he said prompting her to say more.

"I found some herbs," she let him know.

"Really? Those are herbs? I don't know how many times I've passed right by those without really looking at them."

She turned to look at him to see if he was serious. The look on his face was serious. He was looking at the herbs she had found. Adding these to what he had already found would enhance the flavor of all of their meals. Then she spotted the peppercorns. He definitely hadn't found or recognized this plant. Greedily she picked a few of the peppercorns. One way or another she would get him to show her how he ground up the sugarcane. She needed to know how to grind the pepper.

He collected a few more vegetables, enough to put together a meal, as she gathered some of the herbs to season them. The first chance she could get, she knew she was coming back with bowls or other containers to gather more and keep them sorted. Figuring out a way to label them would be really nice too.

When they returned to camp she took over preparing dinner while he built up the fire. They ate and relaxed after dinner. Sitting by the fire she looked up to the stars letting her thoughts move freely. He planned it out so he could take a day off like this. In fact, if she understood what he told her, he did this once a week. It felt so good to take a day off. She knew in truth she had taken several days off for her leg to recover, but before she got hurt, she was busy every day with survival. It was grueling and left her tired almost every day.

She could get used to this pace. She could get used to working with him. He wasn't saying anything, but he was sharing with her. Men so often could get past something without actually having to say it, and that was how he was acting. Like he didn't want to talk about their past, but rather just work with her for their mutual survival. For months she lived here not knowing about the pools and the garden. Two things that made living here better. She considered asking him if they could go get the remainder of her things and bring them to camp, but the sun was setting and he was sitting so quiet and peacefully. She didn't want to interrupt his thoughts, or interrupt the moment.

It was enough to know he was accepting her now. It was sad that she nearly had to die for him to realize they needed to work together, but for now she would accept it. If he didn't want to talk about it, then she could accept that too. Survival was so much more important than worrying about their past relationship. That was the past and it was over with. In the here and now she was ready to work with him, to stay here to help him and let him help her in return.

The sun was down, leaving everything in dusk. Full dark was approaching soon. She looked around and saw a blanket hanging from the now shadowy branches. The clothes were definitely dry now. She grabbed her crutch and pulled up to gather the blankets and clothes. She had the first blanket in the cave when Frank appeared behind her with another blanket, and their clothes. He took a moment to fold the clothes and separated them, placing hers next to the blanket she had just laid down for sleeping. By the time they finished, it was fully dark. If not for the light from the fire, they would have had to wait until morning to bring in and fold the dry clothes.

He stood and turned to leave the cave. "Frank." She stopped him before he could leave. He turned to listen. She couldn't see his face because the fire was behind him. "Where do you sleep?"

"I, um, have a spot out there." He answered. His voice seemed cautious or guarded.

"But," she paused for a moment, "but this is your cave."

"Yes." He continued before she could tell him he could stay. "I'm ok. You needed to sleep here while you recovered, and you still need more time to recover."

He was right that she needed more time to recover. She couldn't deny that fact. "Ok. Yes, but that doesn't mean you have to be kicked out of your own cave."

"I'm not kicked out. I did what needed to be done." His words were so simple and straight forward. He didn't feel that she had put him out, but that he took her in of his own free choice.

"You can stay." She felt like she was pleading, and hoped he didn't hear that in her voice.

Despite the failing light, she could see him lower his face and shake his head, "no, I can't."

"Frank. I don't mind. And there is enough room here for both of us."

He continued to shake his head, "I can't Michelle. Please don't ask. This is something I can't do." His voice filled with emotion as he spoke and before she could think of anything else to say he quickly turned and walked out of the cave.

She almost called out to him, to ask him to come back, but she restrained. She knew she could get up and try to follow him, but once again she restrained. She couldn't think of what she had done wrong to drive him away. They were doing so well working together, and it wasn't right for him to sleep outside instead of staying in his own cave. Fitfully she laid down to sleep, tossing and turning as she tried to think of what she did wrong the past few days. As she tried to think of what would convince him to return to his own cave.

> So tear me open, pour me out
> There's things inside that scream and shout
> And the pain still hates me
> So hold me, until it sleeps
> - Until it Sleeps by Metallica

When she opened her eyes to morning, the sun was well up and bright. She felt tired and sore and knew she had slept later than usual. Outside the cave she could tell Frank had already gone out fishing or gathering for the next meal.

She quickly ate her morning fruit, gathered the empty cups and bowls she could find and placed them in the pouch he had fashioned from one of his shirts. She had everything she needed to gather the herbs found yesterday. Excitedly she went quickly to the garden, planning to explore every plant and know as much about what was there as there was to know. The garden was as much a treasure as when she first found the grove. She identified at least a dozen different plants and a dozen herbs. None of the vegetables were ripe, but they would be soon enough. The herbs were more than ready for harvesting. As she carefully cut the leaves and stems she wanted to harvest she heard her stomach grumble. Hours had passed since breakfast and she was hardly aware of the time spent going through the garden. She needed to finish gathering the herbs and return to camp.

A strong wind blew through the trees overhead as she worked. It was enough to blow her hair into her face as she worked. With hardly a thought she pushed her hair back behind her ear and continued to work. When she finished the pouch hung heavy at her side. The wind blew through the trees in an ominous way. The sun was shining still, but she smelled the moisture in the wind. Quickly she returned to camp with her harvest. Frank was nowhere to be seen as she took the herbs into the cave. She didn't bother to pull them from the pouch, just setting it down and going back out of the cave. He was still out there somewhere. Surely he knew the storm was coming.

When she looked down the trail she saw him coming up the trail at a near run. His breathing was fast and ragged. She got out of his way to let him pass, then followed him. He threw three crabs onto the cutting table and ran into the cave. She checked and found the crabs were already dead. He returned moments later empty handed. His fishing spear and pouch left in the cave.

She met his eyes when he came out. He looked determined, maybe a bit concerned. "I think it's going to be a bad storm. We should move as much as we can into the cave." He said.

She nodded and began gathering things from the cutting table to move them into the cave. The crutch made the task more difficult. Frustrated she dropped it on the bed and went back out to gather things to bring in. The muscle remained weak, but it held as she worked.

He moved wood into the cave by the armloads. Building the stack inside the cave while emptying the stack by the fire pit. The winds grew stronger as they worked, and the first clouds covered the sun, turning the sky to grey. They entered the cave to sort through everything brought in. It was another few minutes work that went quickly as they worked together. The first fat drops of rain fell as they finished up.

"Looks like we made it just in time." She couldn't help but say as they both looked outside the cave. The wind whipped the tops of the trees and the rainfall fell harder as they watched.

"Yeah. It's going to be a bad storm. I should have paid attention this morning, the birds were too quiet."

She didn't respond. There were no other words to add to what was already spoken. The inside of the cave was dry and protected them from the wind blowing outside. As she watched outside she realized it was growing darker. It was only the middle of the day, but if this storm continued to grow worse it would be dark as night. She didn't like the idea of losing their only light, but there wasn't anything to be done about that.

He squatted and cleared an area of rocky ground as close to the entrance as he dared. She turned and watched and realized he was making a fire pit. They were going to have light, and they could cook the crabs he caught that morning. For a moment she wanted to grab him and kiss him. He was doing exactly what they needed the most.

In moments he was shaving the wood to create the tinder he needed to get the fire going. She sat down, pulled out her knife and began working with him. The light continued to fade and she wanted a fire before it became too dark for either of them to see well enough to light one. Their pile of wood shavings grew steadily. She pulled bark apart, separating the fibers to create a dry wadding that would catch easily, but burn quickly.

He grabbed the wadding, the shavings, and the smallest twigs he could find and began building them into a bundle to catch sparks. His flint and steel was still in good shape when he brought it out and began working to light the fire. The light had faded so much she could easily watch the sparks falling into their wadding of tinder. When one landed and held, she blew gently. It grew brighter and moved into the wadding. Smoke began to pour from the wadding, she blew a little more and the sparks ignited into small flames.

They had a fire. Carefully he took over tending to the fire and building it. The larger sticks seemed to take forever to catch, but they did. The fire grew until it was big enough to provide light and warmth in the cave. Warmth that let her know the temperature had fallen as they worked. She didn't notice it until now because they were so busy working to take care of their things.

Thunder rumbled outside. Lightning was moving in close enough to be heard over the wind. They both moved back onto the blanket, sitting with their backs against the solid wall of the cave. They didn't have anything else to do. They just sat there and stared out into the storm until their stomachs grumbled and reminded both of them they had not eaten lunch. She couldn't suppress laughing. They were safe. She was safe. She didn't have to huddle in her cave in the dark during this storm. He had taken care of her again and kept her safe from the tempest raging around them. He started to get up, but she stopped him. "I'll get it, you deserve to relax."

He smiled and nodded wordlessly. She got up without the crutch. Still limping, but able to move, and retrieved his pouch. Inside were the fruit and nuts she expected to find. She pulled the stacked cups and bowls from the other pouch. The topmost bowl and cup were empty of any herbs, their only job was to act as lids for the cups and bowls below them. She transferred a cup of parsley to the empty bowl and took the two cups to be filled with water.

They ate and watched the storm rage outside. Flashes of lightning lit up the sky and trees. The blowing wind whipped leaves until branches broke and crashed to the ground in sodden heaps. The camp was going to be a mess when this storm blew past.

After nearly two hours of silence, she needed something. They didn't have cards or games to play, and she couldn't sit here only watching the storm blow for the rest of the day. "Did I do or say something wrong yesterday?"

He turned to face her, as if taking a moment to read her face before he answered, "no, why do you ask?"

"Last night. I'm probably overthinking things, but when you didn't stay, I didn't know if it was because of something I said or did yesterday."

His face took on a serious look. "We're trapped here by this storm. Maybe we shouldn't talk about this."

So there was something. Something they needed to talk about so they could really work together as a team and survive until they could figure out how to get back home. "Ok, but maybe we should talk about it sometime. Whatever it is, I'm sure we can get past it. You know, we're not just stuck in here because of the storm. It's the whole island we're stuck on."

"Yeah, I know. You don't have to remind me." He replied as he got up to put another log on the fire. He kept it intentionally smaller than he would have outside the cave.

Somehow they managed to change the topic of conversation. They passed the time playing word games and telling stories from their pasts. The storm was calmer by the time they were ready to cook the crab for dinner. Once again she took over, letting him know it was her turn to be productive. She couldn't help but wish something had been ripe in the garden. The rain outside the cave fell steadily onto a mess of fallen leaves and branches. It wasn't as dark as earlier, but it was dark enough as she fixed their dinner.

After eating, they went back to sharing stories and playing word games to pass the time. Outside the rain grew steadier, then the wind and lightning returned. If anything the storm seemed to grow worse. They paused to try to look outside the cave. Flashes of lighting revealed wind whipped trees and a torrential downpour of rain.

"I think you should stay in the cave tonight." She knew she probably shouldn't have said anything, but the words came out before she could stop them. She needed him to talk about what was wrong, to let it out so it could be let go. Maybe having him trapped here in the cave with the storm raging outside wasn't the best time to talk about it, but if they didn't talk now while they obviously had time to talk, then when? He could easily avoid talking to her about anything as long as they had things to do.

"I think this time I won't argue with you." He responded. "I can sleep over here on this side of the cave," he pointed opposite from where she slept.

She looked at the rocky ground he pointed at. She couldn't imagine anyone sleeping on those rocks. Even if he managed to move them around enough to make a somewhat smooth place, he was going to be trying to sleep on lumps. "You can't sleep there."

He leaned back against the wall of the cave, his eyes still looking outside. "I'll be fine, I've been through worse."

"We need to talk about this Frank. I can't keep doing this. I'm glad we are working together and not fighting, but I know something is wrong and I don't even know what it is. I don't know what I said, or what I did since you brought me here, but I can't keep wishing I knew what it was." The need to know filled her heart and mind, pushing the words out. She couldn't stop them now or take them back.

"You haven't said or done anything wrong since I brought you here to my cave." He replied.

"Then what is it Frank. Why do you leave every night even though this is your cave?"

He didn't answer right away, leaving the cave filled with the sound of wind, rain, and thunder. "Every day since I saw you here I have walked past and looked at the tree on the way to the beach. The white scar is still there. It never changed." He answered.

"You mean this is because of what happened so long ago? But you saved me, you saved my life. I thought things were different. Why?"

He sat up and turned to face her, "I was the one who found her." His voice filled with emotions he couldn't hold back. "She was in our bed laying there peacefully, and she was already gone. I called for an ambulance, and I tried to do CPR, but it was too late. She was gone, and I had to take care of everything. I had to arrange the funeral. I had to talk to my son. I had to talk to her family. I didn't get to just stop and cry for the woman I lost. I had to take care of it all.

"If you really want to know why I saved you, it's because of her. I couldn't save her. I wasn't there in time. I had no choice but to watch her die and then deal with the aftermath of her death. I found you and you weren't dead. This time I didn't have to watch someone die and I didn't have to deal with the aftermath of that death. I saved you because I couldn't bear to deal with death again."

He spoke of his late wife. She knew the story. She remembered the times he cried on her shoulder over his loss. She was there for him, helping him through those dark days after his wife died. He should be doing better now, but the tears streaming down his cheeks spoke of a depth of pain she barely understood. Silence stretched between them as she worked to gather her thoughts. He wiped his tears away and went back to leaning against the wall.

"The way you say you saved me makes it sound like you don't care about me," she couldn't hide the sadness over that thought.

"The truth is that I don't like you. I did everything I could to avoid being around you right up until I found you unconscious. After that I stayed as close as I needed to stay to make sure you would survive. But I couldn't sleep here while you were here." His words hit her heart like a rock.

"Why Frank? What did I ever do that was so wrong that you hate me after all these years? We weren't right for each other. I shouldn't have fallen in love with you while you were grieving for the loss of your wife. I shouldn't have let you fall in love with me, but it happened. It just wasn't right. I had to move on, and you needed to move on too."

"I'm not talking about the breakup. I've had my share of those. The reason I don't like you as a person is because you went to Mexico."

"Frank, I told you a.."

"Please don't try to tell me that again!" His voice grew louder in the small confines of the cave. "I know what you said. I know the excuses and the justifications. I sent you money to fly back out to see me and you used that money for your trip to Mexico. I don't care what bills you say you spent the money on. I sent you money for all the bills you told me about that we ended up sharing. You had no right to take money I sent you for a plane ticket to visit me, and then take a vacation to Mexico instead.

"You didn't just hurt me when you did that. You hurt my son. I never should have sent that money to you. I know that now. I didn't know you were the kind of person who could ever do something like that. That's why I don't want to be around you. That's why I don't want you here. Maybe I'm doomed to never be rescued from this Island and I have wished so many times that it was anyone but you here."

She couldn't even speak after listening to the torrent of his words. The anger and hatred were so clear and unmistakable. She couldn't hear the wind, rain, or thunder the whole time he spoke.

He got up while she sat there quietly and he ran out of the cave.

She sat there stunned, then yelled, "Frank! No! Frank get back in here." She got up and looked outside, but in the rain and darkness she couldn't see anything. She called out and yelled for him, but heard only the rain and wind.

She went back and grabbed her crutch to follow after him, when she got to the mouth of the cave everything turned blue with a flash of lightning just outside the cave. The thunder hit immediately and shook her to her core, leaving her ears ringing. She shook her head to try and clear it, and despite the ringing in her ears, she heard the crashing of a tree nearby, but she couldn't tell where it came from.

Stunned she fell back into the cave and huddled against the wall. All of the feelings of safety fled as she looked out at the raging storm. Where was he? Why did he have to run out like that? She cried as she worried that he would be ok. She cried because she couldn't chase after him and make him come back and stay safe. She cried because he hated her so much he would rather run out into a dangerous storm than stay here. She cried until her body shook from the racking sobs. She cried until she fell asleep exhausted.

> The pain that grips you
> The fear that binds you....
> Can't wash it all away
> Can't wish it all away
> Can't cry it all away
> Can't scratch it all away
> - Understanding by Evanescence

Everything was a mess. Inside the cave the blanket was a bundled mess around her legs and her eyes were red and sore from crying. Outside the ground was covered with leaves and branches torn away by the storm and left to fall where they may. Light rain continued to drench the ground. The worst of the storm seemed to be past, leaving the day grey and dreary. Frank was nowhere to be seen, reminding her of the mess their relationship had become. He really did hate her, and he always had. Whatever his reasons for saving her life, they were his own, but it didn't change the fact that he hated her.

Only a few bites of food remained. It wasn't much, but she ate it for breakfast hoping he would go to the grove to get more. She wasn't thinking that she wanted him to get her something to eat, just that she didn't want him to come back and find that she had eaten the last of the food they had in the cave.

The rain continued unabated as she sat there watching it. The few bites she ate were not enough, and her stomach complained even though she didn't feel like eating. She knew it was because of the heaviness in her heart. Her stomach just wanted to be filled regardless of how she felt. The best she could guess was that it was mid-morning. She hated that he still had not returned. Thoughts that he could be out there somewhere hurt and unable to return tried to invade her thoughts, but she pushed them away. He had to be ok. How could she possibly help him like he helped her?

She got up and stepped out of the cave. The rain was cool, but not uncomfortable, with the exception that it was wet. She turned to survey the area around the camp. It looked like everything was covered with broken branches and wet leaves. The cutting table was nearly buried. She turned further and saw what caused the crashing sound she heard the night before. Two trees were down and blocking the path down the hill. She leaned on her crutch and went to them, silently praying that he wasn't there under those trees.

She couldn't see him under them or anywhere around them. Once again she saw no trace of him. Whatever tracks he left were long since washed away. The trees were a problem though. She was on the uphill side of them. If she tried to climb over them, and succeeded in not breaking an arm or a leg, she would likely fall off on the other side and down the hill. She leaned forward onto the first log with both hands. It was higher than her waist.

The image of Frank chopping through the down tree on the trail below came back to mind. The first storm to pass through downed the tree blocking the path to the grove. It wasn't a large tree, and he probably could have gone over it any time he wanted, but he took the time to cut it away. The axe was inside the cave. They took it inside yesterday with all their other possessions they needed to protect from the storm.

She returned to the cave and retrieved the axe. She didn't think about how much her heart hurt because of him. She didn't think about what he did or did not deserve. She simply brought it back out, rested the crutch against a nearby tree and took the first swing. She felt unbalanced and far from graceful. When he swung the axe his body was so smooth and fluid, the axe moved and chopped at his will. She pulled it back, adjusted her balance and swung again.

Frustration wanted to build up as her strike barely dented the wood. She pushed it down. She could do this. Where she lived, everyone who was big enough to hold an axe learned how to chop wood. It was part of survival. The winters there would kill without a thought. Everyone had to be able to cut their own wood and build their own fire if they expected to survive an unexpected power outage. She adjusted again and swung again. The edge bit into the wet wood. Now she knew how to stand. She had to compensate her weight to her right leg and maintain balance, but she knew how to do that. Years of yoga practice were about to pay in dividends.

She swung again and again. Chips of wood began to fall away as she worked. Her shirt was soaked through and clung to her skin. Her hair kept getting in her face, but she pushed it away and continued. The task took over and she worked on that task. She didn't want to think. She just wanted to cut this log and clear the trail down the hill. The muscles in her arms and back responded with her, as if they wanted the log cut away as much as she did. The first crack from the log didn't come as a surprise. She saw it bending, ready to break away as she worked.

When it gave though, it did come as a surprise. It still looked strong enough to hold, but it gave up with the right side falling away and the left rising up a few inches. Had it been the only log, the trail would be clear enough to get past for now. The next one was lower down. Instead of starting on it though, she took a break to get a drink of water. She may not have something to eat, but she did at least have water to keep her mind off food. It was temporary. Once past here she could make her way to the grove and get something to eat. Then go back to crabbing and fishing.

She stopped when she realized she was already thinking in terms of not having Frank to take care of these things. It was true though. This was his cave. Most of the things inside were his things that he had put together for his survival. He was supposed to be here, and she wasn't supposed to be here. Even if they were both stuck on the island, this was his part of the island. She had her own part, her own cave. She had things there that she had put together for her survival.

She had to go back to her cave and her things because...because he hated her. A sob welled up and released as that thought went through her mind. How could she have screwed up so badly that he hated her? She remembered the money he talked about. She almost didn't keep it, but for whatever reason she did keep it. The bills had to be paid and it was all she had to pay them with. Then when he attacked her, calling her every name imaginable she didn't care that she had spent the money. If he was going to be that way, then he deserved to lose the money.

That wasn't right though. He deserved to be angry with her for taking his money and going to Mexico. He deserved to call her those names. What kind of a person was she for thinking she ever had any right to take that money like she did? She took money from a man who lost his wife less than a year before. She took money from a man who struggled to take care of his son on his own. No she didn't spend it in Mexico, but she still spent it.

She couldn't give it back to him either. Of all the things in her duffel bag, she didn't have any money. It wouldn't matter if she did, he couldn't spend it on anything. She knew that didn't matter either. She didn't have the money anyway. She could barely pay her bills each month. She just didn't have a way to pay back what he sent to her.

The axe rested against her leg as the tears began to dry up. She realized the rain was now a slow drizzle. He might not accept it, but she could try to repay him here.

She could find a way to do things for him until the debt was paid. She picked up the axe and went back to cut away the other log. Once again she got in a rhythm of swinging. Once again the wood chips fell away with each swing. This time it was not a surprise when she cut through the log.

She sat down for leverage and pushed against the right side with her feet. The log moved, sliding down the hill until it was clear of the trail. She smiled in triumph. She did it. She really did something useful. With arms tired and sore she went back to the cave to get the pouch. She debated carrying the axe with her, but she knew if she came across any more down trees they would have to wait. She wasn't up to cutting through any more logs.

When she got back to the trail she realized she wasn't using the crutch. It still leaned against the tree where she left it that morning. The weak sunlight through the grey clouds above indicated it was past midday. She considered leaving the crutch, but realized her leg may not be as ready as she thought and climbing back up the hill on a lame leg would be a challenge. She grabbed it and began walking.

She watched everywhere as she walked, hoping she would see him on the trail. She watched her feet as best she could to make sure she didn't trip. Leaves covered the trail, hiding potential hazards and sometimes creating slippery spots. She made it down the hill without incident, turned and began walking to the grove without pause.

Part of her wanted to stop at her cave just to see her familiar place, but she needed something to eat first. She also worried about where Frank was, so she walked past barely looking as she did. If he was hungry he would go to the grove too. It was the only source of readily available food that she knew of. The garden would provide, but unless the vegetables were ripe, they would have to wait. She walked as briskly as she dared on her leg. The muscle began to burn with exertion, but it held and she continued.

She couldn't hide the feelings of disappointment when she didn't see him in the grove. The ground was littered with fruit knocked down the night before. Most of this was going to go to waste, there was nothing either of them could do about it. Some of the trees were stripped of almost all of their fruit, while others with smaller fruits still had some that were not ripe enough to fall.

She stopped to eat, then filled the pouch to capacity and headed back to the camp. Once again she resisted the temptation to stop at her cave. She didn't have anything in there she needed. Her clothes and blanket were at Frank's cave, and she would be returning to her cave soon enough. She went past on the hope that he would be back. That she could see he was unhurt. He didn't have to say anything, he just had to be ok. Right now she needed him to be ok more than anything else.

Climbing up the hill she used the crutch like a walking stick, the burning in her left leg grew as the muscles pushed through exhaustion to get her up to the cave. She refused to give in to the weakness or the pain because she needed to see Frank, and he had to be back. He couldn't stay away from his own cave, from the things he needed to survive.

He wasn't there. Everything was the way it was when she left. Crestfallen she took the fruit to the cave to put it away. He would return and she intended he would have something to eat when he did.

She peeled off the wet shirt and laid it across a rock to dry, then pulled out the towel and dried off. She pulled on dry shirt. When she sat down, the fatigue in her muscles came up with a vengeance. She had pushed herself hard to cut through the logs and go to the grove. That was more exercise than she normally got, even when she took the aerobics classes. She didn't have a choice though. She massaged the muscle in her leg, pushing the tension to release and the blood to flow through. It seemed it didn't want to release, but it did feel better for the massaging.

She noticed the light was growing less. It wasn't late enough for the sun to set, so that could only mean the clouds were building up again. As if summoned by her thought, the rain began again. Fat drops that fell straight down. The wind didn't rise up with the rain, but in moments it was raining steadily, the drops creating their staccato of sound as they hit the wet leaves and rocks.

There were still some warm coals in the fire pit inside the cave. She pulled out her knife and began working on shaving tinder to rebuild the fire. She worked steadily, the weeks of practice evident in the strokes of her knife. The pile of shavings grew quickly. In minutes she had everything in the pit and blew gently to get the coals to ignite the tinder. Smoke quickly rose and was soon replaced by flame. She added wood and built up the fire until it was as big as she wanted.

The yellow light filled the cave and extended out of the cave a short distance. Beyond that it became too dark for her to see. It wasn't fully dark out yet, she knew it only seemed dark because she was sitting close to the fire.

He was out there somewhere still. The fear of him out there hurt couldn't be held back any longer. He should have returned by now. The only reason he wouldn't come back to his cave to get his fishing gear, or his pouch for gathering would be if he was hurt. He needed those things every day to survive and he knew it. He knew what he needed as surely as she did.

She imagined him in the jungle under a broken tree, or maybe he went the other way and he had fallen off the trail and was unable to get back up to the trail. She added wood to the fire, keeping it going, and imagining the horrible possibilities of what could have happened to him. As she thought about them, she promised herself she would find a way to make it up to him. He just had to be ok somehow and she would find a way to make it up to him for taking his money. She would find a way to make it up for hurting him. She would find a way to repay him for saving her life. If there was anything at all she could do for him, she would do it. He just needed to be ok and to come back.

Night darkened everything outside the cave, leaving only the firelight. She kept the fire going though, hoping he would see the light and find his way back. She worried for him. She thought of the person she was, wishing so much she could be better. She didn't want to be the person he saw when he looked at her. She didn't want to be someone who would take another person's money selfishly. She didn't want to be someone who deserved to be hated.

> I can't run anymore,
> I give myself to you,
> I'm sorry, I'm sorry
> In all my bitterness,
> I ignored
> All that's real and true
> All I need is you,
> When night falls on me,
> I'll not close my eyes,
> I'm too alive
> And you're too strong
> I can't lie any more
> I fall down before you
> I'm sorry, I'm sorry
> - October by Evanescence

The rain continued steadily several hours into the night before it finally slowed and stopped. She couldn't sleep, every time she closed her eyes she saw images of him out there wet and hurt, possibly dying. Somehow she did sleep though. When she woke a few embers remained where the fire was, but the sun was up. The light filtered through white clouds, a few patches of blue revealed through small gaps in the clouds. When the sun hit the ground, patches of wispy steam rose into the air.

Nervously she grabbed her crutch and went out to search for him. Worry pushed her harder than any hunger she had felt since arriving on the island. The muscle in her left leg wanted to cramp up and hold her back, but she refused to let it. She could walk all day on the crutch if she needed to. She didn't know which way to go. She didn't know if she should go to the falls or down the hill.

She turned and he was there. Her legs almost gave out seeing him standing at the top of the trail down the hill. He was looking at the logs she had chopped away and didn't see her yet. She couldn't speak though. A lump filled her throat. She moved though. The crutch fell away and the cramped leg seemed forgotten as she moved until she got to him. He turned to her before she got there. She couldn't stop herself from grabbing him, from touching him and knowing that he was ok.

She felt him stiffen at her touch.

"Oh God. I'm sorry. I was just so worried you were hurt. I didn't mean to. I'm just sorry." She let go and her leg chose to give out in that moment. She started to fall and reached out to grab his arm. She caught his arm and barely held her balance.

He held her. She realized his other arm was behind her back helping her get her balance. He didn't say anything. He just stood there, solid as a rock, his face emotionless as he kept her from falling. She managed to get balanced on her right leg. "I'm sorry. I think I pushed it too hard yesterday."

He looked down at her leg. She held the knee bent, letting it rest on her toes. She could feel the throbbing pain through the calf. She knew if she could just rest a bit she would be ok, and the muscle would be stronger for the exercise. It wasn't a bad kind of pain, but it was enough to keep her from putting weight on that leg.

He still didn't say anything, and he kept his emotions hidden from her. It didn't matter though. He was here. He wasn't hurt. The thought barely crossed her mind when she saw the scratch across his chest. It wasn't bleeding, but the dried blood around it indicated it must have bled quite a bit.

"Can you walk?" He finally broke his silence.

"If you can get me back to my crutch, I think I can manage." She wanted to ask what he wanted, but kept the thought to herself.

He moved and she didn't have a choice but to move with him, mostly hopping and using him for balance. He picked up the crutch while holding her steady and she gladly accepted it. Once she was leaning on the crutch he went into the cave, she started to follow, but something about his demeanor made her pause. He seemed so cold now. It was like the fire of his anger burned away and left nothing behind to feel for her. She didn't sense his hatred or animosity, nor did she sense any concern for her safety or well-being. When he kept her from falling, it seemed like an automatic response. It was something he just did.

He came back out carrying his fishing spears and eating a piece of fruit he retrieved from the pouch. He caught her eye as he went past her, but he didn't say anything or nod. He just walked past and went down the trail.

She had no idea until now that it could be any worse. Her heart sank into her stomach as she stood there. She hated when he yelled at her in anger. She hated the way he treated her for so many months, and right now she almost wished he would be that man again, instead of the cold heartless creature she somehow had caused him to become. Numb inside she sat down on the wet leaves and massaged her calf until the cramp released. Then stretched and got it to loosen up even more. Inside she still felt shaken by his behavior. Somehow she pushed those feelings down. She couldn't force his actions, just try to accept them and do what she needed to do. That last part wasn't as easy as it sounded. If she was going to repay him for saving her life and pay him back in some way for the money she took, then somehow she was going to have to communicate with him, and find a way for him to accept her efforts.

She knew now she was well enough to walk to the grove and more. It was time to return to her own cave so he could have his cave back. The thought that this might be her last day here gave her pause and she looked around as if to try and remember it. Looking at it reminded her how much of a mess it really was though. This camp wasn't supposed to look like this. He kept it neat and organized. It may not be much, but this was something she could do for him, and she was not going to let pain in her leg stop her.

She pulled up on the crutch and set about the task of cleaning the camp. All of the broken branches, leaves, and brush she piled up next to the wood pile. Several trips later she brought out all the items they kept outside. Including refilling the water pitchers. A flat stone helped her clean the muddy ash out of the fire pit.

The toilet area was as much of a mess as the rest of camp. She had to return to camp to get the axe and chop away several branches so she could remove the debris for him. This was one luxury she was going to miss very much until she could figure out how to set up something for herself. This and the warm pool she soaked in. For now that belonged to him and she couldn't ask for him to share it. Hopefully he would be willing to share the garden. She could get by without soaking in warm water, but she did need to eat. All she could do is ask and hope for the best.

The time passed as she worked. She managed to keep her weight off her left leg by either hopping or using the crutch. Spots of sunlight came through breaks in the clouds, drying the area over the course of the day. When she got hungry she returned to camp to eat. Then returned to her work of cleaning up the camp for him.

It looked normal again, like it was supposed to look. She could tell by the position of the sun and the feeling in her stomach that it was late in the afternoon. He was still out either fishing or simply avoiding returning to camp. Either one didn't really matter. She set up and started a fire in the fire pit, then went to the cave to gather her belongings. One blanket, two changes of clothes, a bikini, a towel and her knife she wore around her waist out of habit. This shouldn't be any trouble for her to carry back to her cave on her own.

She spread his blanket over the sleeping area, wrapped hers' up and went back out to wait to see if he would return. The idea of just leaving without saying anything seemed wrong. How did you thank someone for saving your life? How could she thank him for giving her at least a chance to see her family and her home again? As long as she was alive then she had that hope. What words could possibly express what it really meant?

She also knew she couldn't apologize enough for what she had done to him. Maybe someday he really could forgive her, and maybe someday she could forgive herself. For now she stared at the fire wondering what she would say to him the next time she saw him. Everything was ready for her to leave. His camp was neat and clean. Her things were wrapped in her blanket sitting a few feet away. She could wait until close to sunset, but then she would have to return to her cave. She couldn't wait until the sun set and try to walk that trail. It was going to be difficult enough between the crutch and carrying her things, she couldn't wait for darkness.

He returned as she sat there lost in her thoughts, and he brought two fish with him. Each fish was easily enough for either one of them. She couldn't resist looking at the fish with longing. Did he mean for her to stay for dinner? He didn't say anything, didn't even acknowledge her sitting there, or the work she had done to clean up the camp. He went to the cutting table and started working on cleaning the fish. His movements were efficient and he quickly had both fish cleaned, spitted, and roasting over the fire.

He sat down, no expression on his face and stared at the fire and the roasting fish. The silence was horrible. She couldn't think of anything to say that would make a difference. She tore her eyes away from him and they landed on her things waiting for her. The sight of her things made it clear that it was time to go, she knew what she needed to do.

She lowered her head and clasped her hands in front of her. "Thank you for saving me." She couldn't keep the trembling out of her voice. "I don't know what to say for what you really did for me. I've never known anyone who could truly say their life was saved by another person. I don't think thank you is even anywhere near enough to cover it."

He didn't say anything, and she didn't hear him move or shift. She kept looking at her hands, and took in a deep breath to continue, "I'm sorry for what I did." She felt the lump in her throat and the first tears in her eyes. "I wish I could go back and really change things. I wish right now I could make it up to you. If I had it, I would give you every penny of the money back."

The tears began to stream down her face freely. She swallowed and forced her voice to work so she could finish. "I'll go back to my cave tonight. You don't need to be bothered by me being here anymore. If you'll let me though, I will do as much for you as I can. I know it isn't much of an offer, but I want to do what I can to pay you what I owe you, and to repay you for what you did for me. I'll find a way to come up to chop wood for you, or gather fruit or vegetables for you. If you want, I'll come up and cook for you as often as you want.

"Like I said. It isn't much, but you should have whatever I can do for you." The words were out. The tears continued to fall onto her lap. He still didn't say anything. Minutes passed as he sat there silently, and she looked down and sobbed quietly. When he didn't respond, she pulled herself up without looking at him.

She picked up the blanket and balanced it over her shoulder while leaning on the crutch. "Frank. I'm so sorry. I do mean it. Please consider my offer." She wanted to say more, but the lump in her throat grew to the point she had to stop. With tears blurring her vision she began walking slowly back to her cave.

"Voulez-vous coucher avec moi ce soir?" He spoke slowly, the words clearly not his native language.

The blanket fell from her suddenly numb fingers. He remembered. Translated he asked 'Will you sleep with me tonight?' She taught him that phrase in French. It was popular and it was fun, and during their relationship it meant so much between them. He remembered.

She turned, he was standing and looking at her. His expression was soft again. "Voulez-vous coucher avec moi ce soir?" he said again.

"Oui," she barely managed to whisper between sobs, "a thousand times, Oui."

She couldn't believe he asked her to stay, and that she said yes. He was walking toward her. In the space of two breaths his arms wrapped around her shoulders. She couldn't keep it in, the emotions flooded through her heart and mind and poured out in a torrent of tears and sobs against his chest. She was sure she kept saying she was sorry over and over, but the connection between her mind and her body seemed severed by the pain in her heart.

When she finally felt somewhat calm again she became aware of his warm chest against her cheek. It wasn't a dream. He was right here and those were his strong arms around her holding her against him. His chest was a mess from her tears and runny nose and he didn't even seem to notice, she had to see his face. She looked up, and he looked back. Tears streaked his cheeks. He was crying too!

She couldn't resist reaching up to wipe away one of his tears. The salty wetness coated her thumb and it was the most amazing thing she could have imagined feeling.

He turned his head back toward the fire and she looked back with him. The fish was still roasting. He let go, squeezed her arm and went to the fire to check on the fish. Even with her nose runny and stuffy she could smell it cooking, which meant is was either done, or nearly done. She wasn't sure if she could trust her legs fully or not, but she didn't have a choice. She walked back and sat down next to the fire.

"Thank you for staying," he said. "I am sure there is lots for both of us to say. Right now though, the only thing I've eaten since the storm is the one piece of fruit."

"I feel like I should go wash my face off. I must look terrible."

"We've both had a rough time."

She scooted over to one of the pitchers of water instead of walking to it. She still didn't trust her feet. The water splashing on her face seemed to wash some of the weight off as it rinsed off her tears. Once the water refreshed her some, she got up and went to her things to get her towel from her blanket. He tended the fish as she scrubbed her face and hands as best she could.

He announced dinner was ready before she was finished scrubbing her face. She was sure she still looked a mess, but dried her face and went back to the fire. He really must have been hungry, he was already well into eating his fish when she sat down. The fish was crispy on the outside, but tender and steaming on the inside and she hardly tasted a single bite of it. Her stomach must have been empty for her to be able to eat anything at all, but she did eat, and had more of it than she thought she would be able to. There was easily less than half of it remaining when she couldn't keep eating. She hated to waste anything, but if she tried to eat more she worried she would become sick.

He finished and rinsed off his hands and face with the water remaining in the jug she filled earlier. The same one she used to wash her face and hands. They sat quietly for a moment. Apparently he didn't know where to begin either. They didn't really look at each other, but they were both aware of each other's presence. He finally broke the silence, "I'm not sure where to begin."

She looked at him, seeing the same sincerity in his face as she heard in his voice. Quietly she moved over to him and sat on her knees in front of him. "I'm sorry. I know I've said that a lot tonight. I just need you to know it. I need you to know that from the bottom of my heart I'm truly sorry I hurt you. I need you to know I'm truly sorry for what I took from you."

She looked into his face as she spoke. Hoping he would see the truth in her eyes.

"That's the first time you truly said that to me. I know you kind of said an apology before, but you didn't say it to me. I really felt like you didn't care about me or about how I felt and what I was going through." He spoke softly.

"I was sorry for hurting you. I should have done a better job of telling you. I didn't realize about the money though. I mean I kind of did, but I didn't at the same time. I know that doesn't make sense, I can barely make it make sense in my own head."

"I think I understand. I've had to apologize before." He was looking directly into her eyes. The firelight danced across his face and she could see his bright green eyes. She felt as though she could see his soul in his eyes, and she wanted him. She wasn't going to make the first move, not after everything that had happened.

"May I kiss you?" His question shook her inside. Was he reading her mind now? Or was he just feeling the same thing she was?

"Yes," she answered as the other questions raced through her mind.

He cupped her cheeks with both hands. He was strong enough he could lift her up to his lips. He didn't though. He simply cupped her cheeks tenderly and bent down to her lips. The space between them felt like an eternity as she worried whether or not she should have said yes. Was she really ready to let him kiss her?

Then his lips touched hers and all thoughts fled. His lips were so warm and soft and so him. She inhaled through her nose and his scent filled her completely. He kept his lips pressed against hers and she didn't want him to stop. Tentatively she placed her hands on his knees, feeling the warm skin and course hair under her fingers and palms. She felt her lips part and his parted with her, she inhaled again, sharply, as his tongue slipped between her lips.

She tasted him. She tasted the fish he had just eaten, and she tasted what made him the man he was. In that taste he could have anything he asked of her. As long as he would give this to her he could ask anything. She leaned into him, pressing harder into the kiss as her body throbbed with desire for him. He responded by holding her face tighter and pressing his lips harder against hers. His breathing quickened against her cheek until she couldn't tell which one of them she heard more.

His skin seemed to grow warmer by the second. She dared to let her fingers move higher up his legs until she felt the denim at the bottom of his shorts. She knew what was there. She couldn't be first to make that move. She wanted to. She wanted to reach up further to feel his arousal. She wanted to free him from his shorts and see him in the firelight. She moved her hands up to his back.

She almost overbalanced on her knees, but he held her firmly.

When she was balanced on her knees again, he released her cheeks and reached under her arms. Without breaking the kiss he picked her up and stood up with her. She barely felt the ground under her outstretched toes and wrapped her arms around his neck to return his kiss. His heart pounded against her chest with the same rhythm of throbbing she felt coursing through all of her body, but especially through her stomach.

He must have opened his eyes, because he turned and with a shuffling walk made his way back to the cave. She knew where they were when he lowered her and laid her down on the blanket in the cave. She almost resisted as the thought that he was being presumptuous crossed her mind. She looked at him though. Inside the shadows of the cave he looked so tender, and the outlines of his muscles, even in shadows were still enticing.

She swore he could have anything he wanted, and she couldn't deny that she wanted him right now. He could be forward, she was his for the taking, and if he didn't hurry and take her, then she was going to take him instead.

He moved over her and kissed again, their tongues meeting in a playful and erotic dance. She ran her hands over his back, his chest, and even his stomach. She wanted to touch him everywhere at once, and was still afraid to push her luck. When his hand pulled up her shirt and touched her bare stomach it was like a miniature explosion that made her entire body tremble with anticipation. His hand moved up, pushing her shirt up ahead of it.

She lost all resistance when his hand found her breast. She reached down to his shorts to find the button and zipper. Impatiently she fumbled to get them unbuttoned and unzipped. Feverishly she pushed the denim down until it was on his legs and he was free. She found him and wrapped her hands around him. The heat from his soft skin infused her entire body.

Her touch erased his remaining patience, he pulled her hands off his body long enough to pull her shirt over her head. While kneeling he grabbed her shorts and pulled them down and off her legs. She had no idea where her clothes flew to and she didn't care. Once naked she grabbed his shorts and made him take them off, once again they went flying and she didn't care where they landed.

She laid back and he followed. She wrapped her arms around his neck and kissed him with uninhibited passion. When she felt him between her legs, she gasped and moaned into his mouth. When he slid into her, slowly and gently she cried out. The first orgasm rolled through her body, and need for him consumed her.

When she felt him fully inside of her, she scratched his back holding onto him so tight. She needed him to stay there for just that moment longer. He couldn't wait though. Something inside unleashed. The gentle man became replaced by a man in need. He pushed up to hold his body above hers and he moved forcefully. She felt the jarring impact of his body over and over and still wanted more. Whatever he wanted or needed was his. She wrapped her legs around him and met his body with her own.

She felt her orgasm coming on strong, and she knew it wasn't going to be stopped or held back. Instinctively she grabbed him, scratching his skin again as it consumed her. All of her mind and heart gave into the orgasm crashing through her body. As strong as it was, she still felt it when he tensed up and released inside of her. She heard his cry of pleasure and her body responded with him again.

It seemed to go on forever, and it lasted the briefest of moments. He collapsed onto her, his strength gone for the moment. She had just enough room to breathe, and he was right where she wanted him to be right then.

They laid there for several minutes just catching their breath. The exhaustion from not sleeping well the past two nights, combined with the emotional exhaustion caught up to her. She was barely aware of his body on hers, but he was there and she was safe.

He shifted so he could lay down on his back, but pulled her over so she could lay her head on his chest. His heart beat sounded so peaceful now. The rhythmic thumping seeped into her mind, sending waves of peace through it. She could feel the world slipping away. Though she could feel him under her arms, and feel his arms around her back, she knew sleep was coming to claim her. She didn't mind though. She was going to wake up with him and they were going to survive this island together.

As she felt the last of her willpower draining away she heard him whisper softly, "It wasn't about you Michelle. It was about me."

His words didn't seem to make sense, and it didn't matter. She let go and fell asleep in his arms.

> Dear, it took so long just to feel alright
> Remember how to put back the light in my eyes
> I wish I had missed the first time that we kissed
> Cause you broke all your promises
> - Jar Of Hearts by Christina Perry

When she opened her eyes, she saw the orange lines created by the streetlight filtering through her blinds. She opened her eyes fully and looked around. The red digits of her alarm clock sitting on her nightstand showed it was almost seven in the morning. The sheets and blankets were still warm from her body and the chill air hit her fully.

"No. Please no," she moaned and grabbed her pillow to stifle her cries as the tears fell from her eyes.

About the Author:

Lee was born in Marietta, Georgia in 1968. He found the love of reading at an early age and quickly read through hundreds of books by dozens of authors.

He is a graduate of Texas Tech University with a Bachelors of Business Administration in Management. His career includes serving his country for eight years in the USAF, computer systems analysis, new project management in manufacturing, and quality assurance in manufacturing.

While living in Horn Lake, Mississippi, Lee gave in to his desire to write the book he had been thinking about for almost a decade. This is where his first novel "Jeremy's Kiss" came to life.

Now living in Vancouver, WA with his wife and kids, his dream of being an author became reality with the self-published release of "Jeremy's Kiss" in 2012. This is Lee's second self-published book. He is currently working on more titles including Natalie's Hunt (the sequel to Jeremy's Kiss) and more.

Follow me on:
My Blog: http://www.leethompson-author.com
Twitter: https://twitter.com/#!/Author_Lee
Facebook: http://www.facebook.com/fleethompson

Made in the USA
Charleston, SC
19 May 2013